"Don't Touch Me," Kalli Snapped. "If You Think You Can Seduce Me Into Agreeing To Sell, You're Crazy."

But Trace just reached out and clasped her waist, pressing her against the kitchen counter. He stepped between her legs, bunching up her skirt, his hands hard and hot on her waist. Then, lowering his face until his nose almost touched hers, he spoke softly, almost menacingly.

"Let's get one thing straight here, sweetheart. I want you. But it doesn't have a thing in hell to do with getting your ranch. If I sleep with you from now to doomsday, I'll still want the ranch. If you never let me touch you again, I'll still want the ranch, and I'll get it."

"I don't want you to touch me." She'd meant it to sound assertive, strong, but it came out wistful.

He smiled. "Liar...."

Dear Reader,

Go no further! I want you to read all about what's in store for you this month at Silhouette Desire. First, there's the moment you've all been waiting for, the triumphant return of Joan Hohl's BIG BAD WOLFE series! MAN OF THE MONTH Cameron Wolfe "stars" in the absolutely wonderful *Wolfe Wedding*. This book, Joan's twenty-fifth Silhouette title, is a keeper. So if you plan on giving it to someone to read—I suggest you get one for yourself *and* one for a friend—it's that good!

In addition, it's always exciting for me to present a unique new miniseries, and SONS AND LOVERS is just such a series. Lucas, Ridge and Reese are all brothers with a secret past... and a romantic future. The series begins with *Lucas: The Loner* by Cindy Gerard, and continues in February with *Reese: The Untamed* by Susan Connell and in March with *Ridge: The Avenger* by Leanne Banks. Don't miss them!

If you like humor, don't miss *Peachy's Proposal,* the next book in Carole Buck's charming, fun-filled WEDDING BELLES series, or *My House or Yours?* the latest from Lass Small.

If ranches are a place you'd like to visit, you must check out Barbara McMahon's *Cowboy's Bride*. And this month is completed with a dramatic, sensuous love story from Metsy Hingle. The story is called *Surrender,* and I think you'll surrender to the talents of this wonderful new writer.

Sincerely,

Lucia Macro
Senior Editor

Please address questions and book requests to:
Silhouette Reader Service
U.S.: 3010 Walden Ave., P.O. Box 1325, Buffalo, NY 14269
Canadian: P.O. Box 609, Fort Erie, Ont. L2A 5X3

BARBARA
McMAHON
COWBOY'S BRIDE

SILHOUETTE *Desire*®
Published by Silhouette Books
America's Publisher of Contemporary Romance

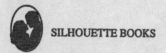

SILHOUETTE BOOKS

ISBN 0-373-05977-9

COWBOY'S BRIDE

Books by Barbara McMahon

Silhouette Desire

One Stubborn Cowboy #915
Cowboy's Bride #977

BARBARA McMAHON

was born and raised in the South. She traveled around the world while working for an international airline, then settled down to raise a family and work for a computer firm. She began writing when her children started school. Now that she has been fortunate enough to realize her long-held dream of quitting her "day job" and writing full-time, she and her husband have moved from the San Francisco Bay area to the Sierra Nevada of California. With the beauty of the mountains visible from her windows, and the pace of life slower, she finds more time than ever to think up stories and share them with others. Barbara also writes for Harlequin Romance.

To Katie and Jessica with love.

One

Trace Longford balanced on the narrow platform of the tall windmill and raised his head. He heard the truck before he saw it. Scanning the area, his gaze swept the grass-covered hills to his left. Beyond, in the distance to the west, the snow-covered granite peaks of the Tetons glittered in the afternoon sun. The truck crested the nearby hill, its engine droning as it slowly crept toward him. Sitting back on his haunches, his arms loosely held on his knees, he watched as the gleaming blue-and-white pickup drew closer and stopped.

Eyes narrowed against the sun's glare, his expression impassive, he watched a small, dark-haired woman climb down from the truck's cab. She tossed back the long braid confining her hair and calmly placed a white Stetson over the glossy black mane. The brim shaded her from the relentless Wyoming sun. Trace watched her look around, catch sight of him on the high narrow platform of the windmill. Raising her chin in determination, she walked over to the base. His eyes never left her as she approached.

"Are you Trace Longford?" she called.

"Yeah." A sudden premonition filled him, made him tense. He wasn't given to premonitions—good or bad—but suddenly he felt a tightening in his gut that presaged trouble. In an instant, he knew her identity. But why the hell she was here, he hadn't a clue. Hadn't she gotten Richard's letter?

"One of the men at the barn told me I might find you here," she called. "Can you come down to talk to me?"

"When I'm done." He didn't like climbing these things in boots and had no intention of leaving before he finished. Ignoring her for a moment, he turned to the last bolt, tightened the nut. That would hold the decrepit blades a few more weeks. The entire windmill needed to be overhauled and new blades installed. But that wasn't his decision—yet. He hesitated a moment before slapping the wrench and pliers into his back pocket and turning to climb down the wooden crosspieces nailed into the structure. Glancing at the woman, he wondered how long she'd stay. And why she'd come out here in the first place. Standing, he reached for the top rung of the ladder.

Kalli Bonotelli watched impatiently as the man returned to his task, ignoring her. Her lips tightened in momentary annoyance, then she shrugged and walked to her truck, leaning against one hot fender, gazing across the acres of green grass spread before her. He probably hadn't a clue who she was. He had a job to do and was doing it. She'd wait. Lifting her eyes, she drank in the beauty of the mountains, hardly able to believe she was finally back. The soft, warm air caressed her cheeks, billowing out her shirt slightly. It smelled so good, clean and dry, carrying the hint of the distant pines and the drying grass of the fields. Totally unlike automobile fumes and smoggy Boston air.

Looking around her, she was almost overwhelmed with the sense of giddy delight that swept through her. She was back! Actually in Wyoming! Standing on her own land. She owned a cattle ranch! She could hardly believe it, though she had all the paperwork to prove it. She'd stopped by the lawyer's office on her way to the Triple T Ranch. It was official. The ranch she'd visited as a child was now hers, Uncle Philip had seen to it.

"Okay, what can I do for you?"

She turned and her eyes widened. He'd climbed down from the platform and was striding easily across the broken ground, his gait smooth, arrogant, almost predatory, like a lobo wolf on the prowl. His jeans molded his long legs, faded almost white at the seams and across the blatant masculine bulge. Scuffed boots encased his feet. His shirt lay tossed across the side of his truck bed.

Kalli swallowed hard and let her eyes drift up his narrow hips, across the hard, flat belly to his muscular chest and shoulders. His skin was as smooth as a baby's, copper in hue, and the musculature clearly defined beneath his taut, tanned skin was perfection. If Michelangelo had sculpted in bronze, this man would have been his masterpiece.

Her eyes clashed with his. Black to black. Locked in an unexpected wave of sensual awareness. Kalli caught her breath, unable to break her gaze. Her breasts tingled, her stomach tightened. Something raw and primitive seemed to stretch between them, and for a split second she forgot why she was here, forgot her delight in the ranch, forgot what she wanted to talk about. She could only feel the shimmering waves of electricity flowing through her, surrounding her. Startled by the strength of the magnetism she could only stand and stare.

"Are you all right? Sun too much for you?" he asked, coming to stand before her, crowding her space. Stealing the air. He tucked his thumbs into the waistband of his jeans, tilted his hips, his stance bold, insolent, cocky. His eyes raked down at her. He stood so close she had to tilt her head to meet his gaze. She wanted to step back. But the side of her truck pressing against her backside prevented that. That, and her pride.

"I'm fine." She took a deep breath. The scent of grass, dust and man filled her nostrils. She held it a moment, reveling in the unfamiliar, exciting odors. Slowly she released it, drew another. Warning bells clanged in her mind. This man was dangerous to her health.

"I'm Trace Longford and I suspect you're Kalli Bonotelli," he said, still watching her warily with his dark brooding eyes. Reaching up to lift his dusty hat, he ran the fingers of one hand through his shaggy black hair, resettled the hat, his gaze never leaving hers. There was no welcome.

She smiled uncertainly. "Yes, that's right. I'm the new owner of the Triple T," she said proudly, holding out her hand.

He took it, released it quickly, not liking the shock of awareness that coursed through him at her touch.

"You're not much bigger than my daughter," he said meeting her eyes again. But she sure filled out clothes better than Becky.

"I know I'm a little on the small side, but my determination is gigantic. The man at the barn said you were acting as foreman of the ranch. I wanted to get settled in the house today, and he said you had the key." Fascinated by the raw essence of masculinity before her, she couldn't resist skimming her glance across his shoulders to sneak another peek at his chest. Perspiration gleamed in the hot sun, the sheen coating his coppery skin with a warm glistening polish.

"I have the key. I didn't know you were coming. Philip died last February. It's May, and I thought by now you'd sell out." He knew there'd been a fair offer on the ranch—he'd made it.

"Oh, no. I just had things to finish up in Boston before I could come. But I'm here for good now." She swept her gaze around the rolling hills, taking in the deep blue sky and the majestic Tetons in the distance.

"For good?" He raised an eyebrow and cast a quick glance over her truck. Obviously new, and packed to the limit with boxes and pieces of furniture. He frowned. He didn't want her staying.

"Yes. For good." She met his gaze, tilting her chin firmly. She could feel his disapproval. But she ignored it. She'd already fought the battle with her parents. The attitude of a stranger fell low on the list of influence. She was here, and here she would stay! At twenty-eight she was old enough to know her own mind. Actually living on the ranch had been her fantasy since she'd been a preteen and first spent the summer with her uncle. She'd spent every minute of five summers following her mother's older brother around, riding the range with him, attending livestock sales, fantasizing about living forever on the ranch.

"What do you know about ranching? Thought you were from Boston," he said, frowning at her.

"I am, but I know enough to get started. I used to live here in the summers. Picked up a few things from my uncle. And I figure you can teach me, can't you?"

"I don't work here." Hell, just what he needed, some city-slicker woman wanting him to do all her work while she reaped all the benefits.

"But the man at the barn said you were acting as foreman."

"Right. Philip was sick for several months before he died so I helped out. When there was no one to run the place after he was gone, I stepped in as acting foreman. But if you're here now, there's no need, right? You're the owner, you run it," he challenged, watching her intensely. He didn't want anything to do with some city woman who thought she could waltz in and take over the ranch after living on it for a few summers as a kid. Hell, it had to have been years ago. He'd have seen her during the past ten years if she'd been here. Let her fall on her pretty face. Then maybe she'd listen to reason about selling. She couldn't have the first idea about running a cattle ranch.

"I'm willing to make the job permanent," she offered, a spark of uncertainty touching her. She'd counted on having a foreman to help run the spread, at least until she knew enough to be totally in charge. If he didn't stay, she wasn't even sure how she'd go about hiring a new foreman.

"Don't need a job," he said, lifting his hat again, tilting it over his eyes when he resettled it. Slowly he moved away, toward his truck. He pulled on his shirt, but left it unbuttoned. If she didn't stop looking at him as if she was about to eat him up, he was going to embarrass them both. He could feel the tightening in his belly. He felt like a randy teenager wanting to show off to a pretty woman, flex his muscles— Whoa! Dammit, he'd just met her. A starry-eyed woman who wanted the glamour of a ranch without knowing anything about the work and hardships involved would prove a definite liability in more ways than one. Hadn't his experience with Alyssa been enough?

"I'll pay top dollar." Kalli grinned. She had always longed to say that. "Please, consider it, at least. Just until I make sure I know enough to run the ranch on my own. I came all the way from Boston and don't know anyone around here who is qualified to run it. The man at the barn—"

"Probably Joshua," Trace said as he leaned against his truck bed and looked at her again. "Tall, thin with gray hair?"

She nodded. "He said—"

"He said I was acting as foreman, you're repeating yourself. That's the way it was, but now that you're here, you can act as your own foreman. I've got a place of my own."

"Please," she said, feeling a touch of panic. "Help me out until I can learn something about this place. If you like, I'll start looking for another foreman right away. You can help me interview. It'll only be for a few weeks." Kalli swallowed, afraid to be alone in this. She knew almost nothing about the ranching business. She had thought to find the place operating along the lines her uncle had run it. She'd wanted to ride, see how cowboys worked and learn as she went along. "I can't even pretend to know enough to run this place right now."

"Sell out. It takes a lot of work and knowledge to run a successful cattle ranch. You don't sit on the porch and watch the money roll in."

She stiffened, a little guilty because that was close to what she'd thought to find. "I know that."

"Wyoming's a hard land. Hot as hell in summer, snow up to your eyeballs or higher in winter."

"Boston has snow," she said stiffly.

"Sure, but have you worked out in it for all hours trying to save your herd? Have you broken ice on the water troughs or river edges so the cattle can drink, only to have it freeze again before a dozen can get a drop? Have you fought for the lives of the calves born early in unexpected spring blizzards? Worried about predators, rustlers and other hazards to a herd that can wipe you out financially in an instant?" Damn, it was a hard life, one a person was born to, not sashayed in to as if it was a walk in the park.

"No, I haven't done any of that. But don't think discouraging me will change my mind. I've always wanted to live here on the ranch and now that I'm here, nothing is going to make me leave. If you want the job, temporarily, it's yours. If not, then I'll thank you for your assistance thus far and bid you goodbye." She tilted her chin as anger flared in her eyes. She knew she had little experience, but she could learn, dammit, and she would!

He hesitated a moment, then shook his head at his own folly. "I'll do it for a couple of weeks," he heard himself say. Hell! He didn't want her getting another foreman. He wanted her gone. He should be in his truck heading for his own place. He had no business tangling up with the new owner of the Triple T. He wanted the ranch for himself, not to run it for some little city slicker from Boston. He looked away, scowling at his reaction to her. The way she filled out those jeans was positively indecent. She shouldn't be allowed outside. He rubbed his hand across his eyes, blinked in the bright sun. She was Becky's size, and as dark as he. He liked tall, leggy blondes. *Yeah, like Alyssa,* he thought sardonically.

"Thank you. Now, the quicker you can help me get moved in, the quicker I'll be able to learn about being a rancher."

"Yes, ma'am." He touched the brim of his hat and climbed into his truck. "See you at the house," he called from the window as he started his truck and drove furiously across the rough track, dirt spinning from beneath his wheels, dust plumes wafting up in the still air.

Kalli watched him drive off, feeling drained from the encounter. She had thought it would be easier to get him to help. Instead, she knew he'd agreed under pressure. And only for a couple of weeks. Hastily turning to her new truck, she climbed in and followed the dusty trail he'd left, her thoughts churning.

By the time she reached the house Trace had commandeered two other men, Josh, whom she'd already spoken to, and José. All three pitched in to unload her truck. In less than half an hour she was moved in. Everything still needed to be put away, but she would do that later, by herself.

"Thank you, gentlemen," she said when the last box was placed in the hall.

"Pleasure, miss." José tipped his hat, then escaped.

Joshua nodded, then glanced at Trace. "That all, then?"

"Yeah. For the time being, I'll be ramrodding this place. Just until Miss Bonotelli comes up to speed or sells. Tell the others, will you?" His eyes danced in secret amusement as he glanced over to his new boss.

Uneasily, Kalli smiled at him and Joshua. "I'd appreciate any help you can give me, too, Joshua," she said, ignoring Trace's comment about selling.

"Yes'm. You'll need it. Takes years to know enough to run a ranch this size," he said dourly.

She blinked. *Years?* She had to learn faster than that. She looked at Trace in dismay. She couldn't be around this disturbing male who was already causing problems with her equilibrium for *years.* She was hoping it would only be a matter of days—weeks at the most. Turning to Joshua, she nodded, hoping her disquieting thoughts didn't show in her face. Had she bitten off more than she could chew?

"Well, then I had better get started, hadn't I?" she said briskly.

"Tomorrow. We'll start tomorrow," Trace said, moving toward the door.

"Why not now?"

Joshua continued out the door while Trace turned. "Because I have things to do. I wasn't planning on you showing up today. You get settled in the house. Tomorrow first thing I'll come by and we can decide what you want to do.''

Kalli wanted to argue, to establish that she was the boss and would give the orders. For that's what his suggestion was, an order. Yet it made sense. She could get settled, get a good night's sleep and be fresh tomorrow when they started. She was tired from driving. And some of the initial excitement was fading as the reality of her situation began to sink in. She needed to recharge and regain her enthusiasm.

''Okay.'' Her eyes strayed to the hair brushing his collar, then down the opening of the cotton shirt, across the smooth expanse of muscles. Down to his hard belly, bisected by the waistband of his jeans. Jerking her head up, she met his eyes. Was that awareness she saw there? Desire? The hot gleam in his dark eyes disturbed, tantalized, drew her.

''I'll be here first thing, have breakfast ready.'' With that he pushed open the screen door and strode across the wooden porch, his boots ringing loudly in the still afternoon air. The footsteps slowly faded as he hit the gravel and then they were gone.

Kalli stared after him. *Have breakfast ready?* Was that part of providing for a foreman? Was he expecting her to do the cooking? For him? For all the hands?

Narrowing her eyes, she turned away. If he thought just because she was a woman that she was going to cook for him, for all of them, he had another thought coming. She was a great cook, but she hadn't left Boston to become a cook at her own ranch. She'd hire someone if they didn't already have a cook. If she could afford it, that was. She sighed, wishing she knew more about the entire setup. She had stacks of papers the lawyer had given her. After she put away her things, she'd start going through them all.

Wishing she'd been more forceful in dealing with her new foreman, she turned around to face the front room, really seeing it for the first time in years. The windows were shaded by the porch roof, yet the room was light and airy and at least twenty degrees cooler than outside. The furniture was heavy, with dark wood and plaids. She and Uncle Philip had spent every evening here. It seemed smaller somehow than when she'd visited as a teenager. She'd have to do something to lighten it up a bit—it was too sturdy and masculine for her. Yet Trace fit right in. The thought came unbidden.

She frowned. She wasn't going to think about Trace Longford any more today. Or her strange reaction to him. She was used to being around men. For heaven's sake, she had five brothers, four older and one younger. And as a nurse, being ordered about by male doctors and interns was enough to cure any woman of early infatuations with men. She had plenty to think about with settling in a strange home, out in the middle of a cattle ranch, miles from stores, theaters and traffic. She didn't need to think about sexy Trace Longford.

The loud pounding on her bedroom door brought Kalli instantly awake the next morning. She sat up, suddenly fearful. Was there a fire? An emergency of some sort? Flinging off the sheet, she hurried to the door and snatched it open. Stunned, she stared at Trace Longford. He was fully dressed, his hat in one hand. Clean-shaven, hair combed, he was obviously ready for work. Leaning on his forearm braced against the jamb, he loomed over her, his gaze raking her as she held onto the doorknob, her heart pounding.

"What's the matter?" she asked breathlessly.

"Nothing, just looking for you, that's all. It's almost six. I came first thing, like I said. Where's breakfast?"

She stared at him. Then looked over her shoulder, out her window. Dawn was just breaking. A glance at her clock showed it was indeed just six o'clock. She turned back in total disbelief.

His eyes skimmed her bare legs. She was suddenly aware of her skimpy sleeping attire. The T-shirt belonged to one of her brothers. Faded and soft after countless washings, it molded her figure like a second skin, ending mid-thigh. Conscious that her hair must be a mess, that she was probably still flushed from sleeping and that there was only the thin layer of cotton between her and this man, she stepped back a foot, swallowed hard.

"I'll be out in a minute," she said and slammed the door in his face as heat and tension filled her. Breathing hard, she tried to infuse some strength into her weak knees. She felt as if he'd touched her with his hands, not just his eyes. Her heart beat rapidly, and her breath came shallow and fast. Heat built deep inside. What would it feel like to actually have him touch her? Run his hard hands up her thighs, pull her hips against his? Feel that warm, smooth copper skin against hers?

"Oh, God, don't let me develop a crush on a cowboy." She turned away to find her jeans and get dressed. Aware that only the thickness of the door separated them, she hurried to the bathroom and closed the door. Locked it. As if that could lock out the images of them tangled together that played in her mind. She really wished she could just touch him for a moment, see if he was as hard as he looked beneath those muscles. See if that skin was as warm and taut as it appeared yesterday in the glittering afternoon sun. Splashing cold water on her face, she tried to drive away the images skipping around in her mind.

When she was dressed in jeans and a yellow cotton top, hair brushed to soft, dark, silky waves caught in a clip and left to hang down her back, she ventured into the kitchen. Trace leaned against the counter, arms crossed over his chest, legs crossed at the ankle, waiting as the coffee machine filtered the brew. The fragrance permeated the kitchen. Sunlight was beginning to fill the room, dust motes dancing in the rays.

He looked up when she entered, his eyes dark and mysterious as he stared at her, not at all embarrassed by taking over her kitchen. By filling it with his presence. His hat rested on the counter. His hair shone as black as her own, but straight, not wavy, with none of the reddish highlights that gleamed in hers.

"Make yourself at home," she said sarcastically.

A smile touched his lips and then disappeared. "Thought you were anxious to start learning how to run a ranch," he said easily, unaffected by her sarcasm.

"I am, but at six in the morning?" she protested.

"There's a lot to do on a working ranch, and in the summer the morning's the coolest time to do it. The men are all up and eating now. Thought we could eat breakfast together and go over what you want done, what you want to learn. Plan the day, then get started. That's what Philip and I did when he was sick."

She knew it made sense, but at six o'clock?

"Who feeds the men?"

"Charlie Pearson. You have four hands. Charlie cooks for all of them in addition to his other duties. Joshua takes care of the horses. José and Tim mostly take care of the cattle, the fencing, the water holes."

"Why don't you eat with them?" She knew she sounded ungracious, but six in the morning wasn't the best time for her. She had never liked early mornings.

"Thought you'd want to discuss some things privately." He shrugged. "If not, we can mosey over there and join them."

She shook her head and gave up. She headed to the refrigerator, then withdrew the eggs and bacon she'd purchased in Jackson yesterday. This one time, she'd cook.

Contrary to what Trace had said, he didn't discuss the ranch over breakfast. He questioned her about Boston instead.

"Why do you want to know so much about me?" she asked fretfully after telling him about her family and her brothers, wishing he'd volunteer something about himself. She wanted to know more about him. About the ranch, she meant.

"Figure if I can understand what experience you've had, I'll know better how to teach you about running a ranch. What did you do before you inherited this place?"

"I was a nurse."

He was surprised. "A nurse?"

She nodded, then grinned. "Does that surprise you? I've been an emergency room nurse for almost eight years."

He stared at her. She was delicate, dainty, pretty. And she was used to the gruesome experiences in a big city emergency room. He shook his head. Philip had mentioned her from time to time. Even saying that he'd left her the ranch, but was sure she'd sell it to Trace. Only she'd refused his first offer and shown up yesterday, ready to stay. Hell, he'd worked the ranch for years, helped Philip out time after time, ramrodded the entire operation since last Christmas, and it all went to some petite nurse from Boston who probably didn't know a steer from a bull from a heifer.

"Can you ride?"

Kalli smiled happily and nodded. "Yes. I told you, I spent summers here when I was a girl."

"From the looks of you, that was some time ago." He didn't know why he wanted to get a rise out of her, but he did.

She carefully placed her fork on her plate lest she be tempted to fling it at this arrogant cowboy. "Actually, I've been riding again in Boston since I learned I was coming out here. I can ride just fine, Mr. Longford."

"We'll see, won't we. And the name's Trace. Just Trace." He finished his coffee and pushed back his chair. He carried his dishes to the sink, then ran water over them and turned to meet her surprised eyes.

"Ready, Miss Bonotelli?"

"The name's Kalli, just Kalli," she sassed back. She caught up her hat and was right behind him when he left the house. She fumed at the way he got under her skin. His long legs ate up the distance to the barn, and she almost had to run to keep up with him. He was doing it deliberately, she was sure.

"Are we in a hurry?" she asked breathlessly.

He stopped and looked at her, not tilting his head, his black eyes narrowed as he took in her situation.

"How tall are you?" he asked.

"Just over five feet two," she replied, using the moment to catch up and take a deep breath. "Not six feet like you. My stride is shorter."

"Yes, ma'am," he murmured, turning to walk slowly toward the barn.

"And you don't need to patronize me, cowboy," she muttered beneath her breath. But she appreciated the slower pace.

She couldn't manage the saddle. It was too heavy and the horse too high for her to get it on. Trace watched her struggle with it for a long moment. When she glared at him, he stepped forward and took it from her, effortlessly settling it on the horse's back. He cinched him up, checked the stirrups and turned to her. "Normally everyone saddles his or her own mount. But since you're the boss lady, I'll do it for you. Need a hand up?"

She hated his patronizing air. Dammit, she couldn't help her size. She had not had to saddle her own horse at the riding academy. Glaring at him, she hesitated. She didn't want him touching her. She was afraid of what her reaction would be. The feelings he stirred in her were unlike any she'd experienced before. Yet she knew she couldn't get in that saddle without some help. The horse was enormous, and the stirrup was almost at shoulder level. She glanced around for something to step on, a mounting block, a stepladder. Uncle Philip had had a platform for her to use. It was long gone. There was nothing else. What choice did she have?

"Very well, thank you." She'd keep it formal. Polite. Not let him suspect for an instant that touching him would have any effect on her at all.

Trace cupped his hands together and leaned over her. Kalli gave him her foot and reached for the saddle horn with one hand. She steadied her other hand against his shoulder, feeling the steely strength of his muscles, the heat from his skin scorching her hand. She lost her concentration when her gaze met his as he slowly straightened and lifted her effortlessly from the barn floor. His dark eyes held hers. The sensations swimming around them, between them, threatened to swamp her. She was lost and had the strongest urge to lean forward the few inches that separated them and lightly touch his lips with hers. Would his mouth be hot and hard against hers, or would he temper his male strength to coax a feminine response?

"Kalli, get in the saddle." His voice was almost hoarse as he held her with his hands beneath her boot, his eyes impaling hers. If she didn't stop looking at him like that he'd kiss her so hard her head would spin. Like his was. As far as he was concerned, the sooner she was gone, the better. He didn't need any sexual overtones in dealing with the lady. He wanted her gone, it was as simple as that.

She scrambled onto the horse, settled in the saddle. The stirrups dangled too long for her short legs. *Damn!*

"I'll adjust them." He wouldn't think of her jean-clad thigh so close he could lean his cheek against it, wouldn't think about her womanly hips at eye level, or the sweet scent of flowers and strawberries that seemed to emanate from her body. He yanked on the strap, settled the buckle and straightened the leather. Taking her ankle in his hand, he threaded her foot into the stirrup. Running his hand lightly up her leg, he tested her seat. His hand burned as he felt the taut muscles of her thigh, imagined it wrapped around him in the heat of lovemaking. Felt the soft curve of her hips as he judged her seat in the saddle. Wished he could feel them beneath him, his hands clasping her.

He heard Kalli draw in a breath, but dared not look at her. As if nothing was wrong, he crossed beneath the horse's head and adjusted the right stirrup, his hand lingering on her thigh, her hip. The painful constriction in his jeans made him pause a moment longer than he wanted. Hell, he had to get away from her before he made a damn fool of himself and couldn't walk.

Her hand brushed against his, trying to dislodge his hold, but her fingers got tangled up with his, and Trace raised his gaze to hers, surprised to note a slight flush across her cheeks, the sparkle in her dark eyes. Her lips parted as she panted slightly in the still morning air.

"I could have done that myself," she snapped, embarrassed at the reaction her body betrayed her with.

Slowly he pulled his fingers from hers, reached out and handed her the reins. He spun on his heel and headed for his own mount.

"Part of the job, ma'am." Dammit, he was playing with fire tangling with this lady. He'd learned his lesson a long time ago. And learned it well. He wouldn't let long-dormant sexual awareness blind him to all good sense. This woman was nothing but a problem. Someone to get rid of as soon as he could. He wanted her land. Nothing else.

Maybe a couple of nights in her bed. The insidious thought came uninvited, unexpected. His entire body tightened in anticipation at the thought. Clenching his teeth hard, he stepped up into his saddle and settled in. Reseating his hat, he nodded for her to start.

Kalli turned her horse and rode quietly from the barn, pausing in the yard, waiting for Trace to join her. When he pulled up beside her, she studied him uncertainly, trying to put the incident behind her. He appeared to have seen nothing unexceptionable in her behavior. And she wanted to keep it that way.

"Which way do we go? I want to see it all!"

He nodded toward the right and they started off.

"I almost didn't come here, you know," she said as her gaze darted avidly in all directions. She turned from time to time to look behind her, wanting to see everything.

"How's that?"

"I had an offer for the place, from a neighbor, the Flying Cloud Ranch. My parents pressured me to accept. It's been ten years or so since I've been here. But I remembered how much I loved it. I always wanted to live here with Uncle Philip, but then I got caught up in nursing and just never found time to come back. I've read every western that's ever been written, from Zane Grey to Louis L'Amour to Larry McMurtry. And I have over seventy tapes of western movies, from *Shane* to *Silverado* to *Lonesome Dove*. God, after inheriting this I just couldn't stay in Boston."

It was even worse than Trace thought. She was some starry-eyed romantic who thought ranching was like a storybook. "It's not like you see in the movies," he warned. "You'd do better to accept my offer, stay a while, then return to Boston."

She was silent for a moment. Had she heard him correctly?

"Your offer? You own Flying Cloud Ranch? You're the one who wants to buy me out?" she asked in disbelief.

He nodded.

"You have a hell of a nerve coming here and pretending to help me out when all along you're trying to get my property!"

"You asked me to stay," he reminded her.

"No wonder you told me I don't belong here—"

"You *don't* belong here," he interrupted. "You're some starry-eyed romantic city girl who thinks the wild West is alive and waiting to fulfill your fantasies. As soon as the novelty wears off, you'll leave so fast it'll make your head spin. I'll try to keep you from running the place into the ground before you leave."

He knew he'd have his hands full convincing her to give up the place. She looked like a kid in a candy store, excited, happy, fascinated. It would be up to him to show her how hard life on a ranch really was, to convince her to sell. To him.

For a long moment he didn't like the idea. She was so happy, he felt almost mean planning to drive her away. Yet he had to convince her to leave. Give it up, sell and return to Boston. He wanted the land, needed this ranch to expand his holdings. He didn't have time for some city woman who fantasized about ranch life.

"You won't stay," he said, knowing he'd make sure, no matter how much her body called to his. When it came time for him to marry again, it would be to one of his own kind, a Wyoming woman born and bred, with a similar heritage, similar outlook and joint future.

God, he wasn't thinking of marrying again! He'd already tried that once, with disastrous results. He'd been without sex for too long if just being around this woman kindled thoughts like that.

"I will stay, Trace Longford. I've wanted this all my life. This ranch was given to me as a gift, and I will treasure it. I don't want your help. I'll find another foreman. But nothing's going to drive me away." With that, Kalli settled her hat firmly and kicked her horse, taking off across her ranch.

Two
***

Trace spurred his horse and caught up with her, settling to match her pace as they flew across the range.

Angrily, Kalli pulled her horse to a walk.

Trace reined in and looked at her. "I'll stay on as foreman until you decide what you want to do."

"I already know what I'm going to do. I don't need you undermining my confidence and trying to get me to sell."

"I won't. I'll show you all I know. It's in both our interests to keep the ranch going in top condition."

Kalli looked away, considering his offer. If he owned the Flying Cloud, he had to know what he was doing. He had enough money to buy her place, if she would ever sell. Could she trust him, however? A sudden unwelcomed thought arose.

"You mentioned a daughter yesterday. Are you married?" Surely he couldn't be. If he was married he wouldn't be putting his hands on her legs, wouldn't have caressed—yes *caressed*—her hip when checking to see if she fit the saddle. At least she didn't think he would have behaved in such a manner if he was married. He didn't strike her as the type to play around. But then, what did she know of him?

"No. Divorced." His gaze touched on her for a moment, then swept across the acres before them. "I assume you're single, as well," he said, not looking at her.

"Yes. Tell me about your daughter." The relief she felt hearing he was divorced was surely too strong to make sense. She just needed him to guide her in running the ranch. If she took him up on his offer. She wasn't looking for an affair with a sexy cowboy. Especially one she was sure didn't like her.

"She's twelve. As tall as you, but not filled out as nicely."

"Does she live with you?"

"Yeah. Her mother didn't want her."

Kalli looked at him in surprise, but he was studying the far horizon. "How could any woman not want her own child?" she blurted out. She cherished the warm ties in her family, the love and affection of both her parents toward all their children.

He looked at her in some surprise. "There are a lot of woman who aren't maternal. Alyssa wanted fast cars and fast men. She had no use for domesticity. No use for a kid. She left us, we didn't leave her. Becky does just fine without her."

"Does she write or visit?" Kalli couldn't comprehend a mother turning her back on her own child. How awful for the child. Did she feel abandoned?

"Haven't heard from her in over eleven years." His eyes narrowed. "Not that it's any business of yours," he said bluntly.

Kalli felt the heat rise in her face. He was right. She was just being nosy. But she was interested. She couldn't understand anyone ignoring her child for eleven years! That meant he had raised his daughter since she was an infant. "It must have been hard on you, raising her all this time, alone."

"I've managed." He bit out the reply, not wanting to admit to her or anyone the tough times he'd had. He'd made it through, and Becky was doing all right, even if he didn't have much idea what to do with a girl child. Before long he'd have to get someone to help him. He knew nothing about dresses and parties. Becky was almost a teenager—she'd be wanting those things soon.

Kalli longed to ask him just how he managed, but his last comment was cold enough to keep the question silent. But she wondered if there was any way she could help him and his daughter, in exchange for his teaching her about the business of ranching. It was an idea. If she allowed him to stay.

"Yonder, part of your herd." He nodded to the field that was just coming into view. Spread out before them stood a couple of hundred head of reddish cattle with white faces grazing knee deep in the tall spring grass.

"What kind of cattle?" Kalli asked, drawing her horse to a stop and gazing at the herd, a feeling of wonder and delight welling up inside her. Her cattle! She was truly on her ranch. Briefly she thought of her uncle. They had not been close except for the summers she'd spent at the ranch. But she still missed him. Giving him silent thanks for leaving her his place, she attended Trace.

"Polled Herefords. Last fall the herd was over two thousand. You need to take a tally soon to count the new calves. Past time for spring branding, tagging and castrating."

"So many?" She bit her lip and studied the cattle. She didn't have a clue what to do with them. What did she know about branding and calving and selling cattle for profit? Nothing. Spring roundups had already been finished each time she came to visit. The magnitude of the undertaking before her began to unfold. She was a nurse, not a rancher. Could she learn enough to run this place? Or would she forever be dependent on men who had been raised in ranching to do the actual work, make the final decisions?

Trace slouched in his saddle and studied the woman beside him. Just maybe she was starting to get a feel for how little she knew. She looked worried as she stared at the cattle. He shrugged. Good, maybe she'd realize it was too much for her and leave.

"Small herd. Needs to be built up. Got any plans for that?"

She flashed him an angry look.

"Of course I don't have any plans. I don't know what I have. I don't know what's expected to run a ranch. Don't you think I need to learn all that before making plans for the future?"

Hot-tempered thing, he thought, almost smiling at her reaction. "Yes, ma'am, I reckon you do. But decisions have to be made *now*. You can't just take off a few months to learn things. Your spring calves are ready to be tagged, branded and castrated. You need to inoculate the herd, check for river ticks, get an accurate count so you can plan which ones to cull for sale now and how many to keep. Plan your breeding, what bulls are you going to use with which heifers. The rotation of the range for maximum buildup on your herd has to be figured and the cattle moved appropriately. The watering places have to be checked, the fencing monitored. We had a lot of snow last winter, some of the fencing's bound to be down. If you don't get it fixed, you could lose cattle, or they could damage another's property and cost you to repair. You need to bring your records up to date, make sure the IRS is satisfied with the estimated taxes." He stopped. Her face was in profile, but he could catch the glimmer of tears shimmering in her eye. She stared over the herd, listening to him enumerate all the things that needed to be done that he knew she hadn't a clue how to handle. Maybe she'd see sense now.

But a small corner of him felt like it had been kicked.

Kalli listened to him go on and on about various aspects of a ranch. She didn't understand half of what he was saying. All she could do was listen as the endless list continued. How could she ever hope to manage a ranch? She was a nurse. She was from Boston, not some wild western town where she might have picked up some aspects of ranching by osmosis. She hadn't a clue, and he knew it. Damn him, he knew it and still continued relentlessly with his list of things to be done.

It hurt. She had been amazed, then overjoyed when she first learned of her inheritance. She had never expected Uncle Philip to leave her anything. Kalli had been quite fond of him, but except for letters and a few phone calls, she hadn't seen him since high school. When she learned she had inherited the ranch in Wyoming, she felt as if she'd won the lottery.

Now she wasn't so sure.

She cleared her throat, refusing to look at Trace, refusing to let him see how overwhelmed she felt. ''Is this the whole herd?'' she asked.

He raised an eyebrow in surprise. He'd expected her to want to go back to the house, think about all he told her and start loading her truck. A glimmer of respect for her began.

''No. Some are over near the Flying Cloud. Come on.'' He started his horse toward the west, kicked him into a lope, and he ate up the distance. The sooner he was finished here the sooner he could get back to his own place.

Kalli was glad for the riding she'd been doing in Boston since she found out about inheriting the Triple T. Otherwise she would never have been able to keep up.

Following Trace, the wind blew the tears from her eyes. She eagerly studied the passing land, searching for a way to remember where she was and how to get home. That much she'd learned from Louis L'Amour.

She also studied Trace Longford. He rode his horse as if he was part of it. His long legs tightened around the saddle, the muscles clearly defined in the indecently tight jeans he wore. His back was ramrod straight, like an arrogant Indian brave of old. Startled, with his copper skin and dark hair, she realized he might be part Indian. Not necessarily, since her own skin was dark, her own hair almost as black as his. But maybe. An Indian. On a ranch in Wyoming. Dare she ask him?

A few minutes later Trace drew to a halt on the top of a small bluff. He swung his leg over his saddle horn and leaned his elbow on it, watching as Kalli drew near. Involuntarily she smiled at the picture he made. Now if he would only pull out a sack of tobacco and roll a cigarette—

"That's the rest of the herd. As far from your house as it can get and still be on Triple T property." The cattle grazed slowly in the warming morning. Beyond them, Kalli could see the endless stretch of barbed wire fence.

"You own the adjacent property?" she asked.

"Yeah. That's why I want your place, to expand."

"I must have other neighbors. I'll have to meet them."

He looked at her with those dark eyes and nodded. "In time. You have too much to do right now. Socializing will have to wait." Alyssa had never wanted to work, she had only wanted to party. When Kalli finally realized she had to work first, she'd be glad to sell the land and return to Boston.

Kalli's temper flared again. How dare he arrogantly tell her what she could or could not do? She was in charge around here, not Mr. High and Mighty Acting Foreman

Trace Longford, and the sooner she made that clear to him the better.

"I'll meet them if I choose and when I choose. What I do with my time is my concern, do you understand, Mr. Longford? You're working as my foreman, not my keeper."

His own anger rose, as much due to the strumming tension being around her caused as the provocative sass of her words. "You listen to me, Miss Boston. You want me to work as the ranch foreman. If you don't like the orders I give, fire me. But if you want to run this ranch, your first responsibility is to learn as much as you can as fast as you so I can quit and get back to my own place. If you have another agenda, then I'll take myself off now and leave you to it today."

His smoldering glare held her captive. The heat radiating from him, the tight line of his lips, the rigid way he held himself under control let Kalli know his temper could match hers any day. Maybe beat hers. She had to face it, she couldn't afford to have him leave. None of the other cowboys sounded as if they knew what to do beyond their own particular jobs. She needed Trace. And he knew it. But she'd watch him, make sure he didn't make things more difficult for her. Though she couldn't imagine things being any more difficult. The task ahead was monumental.

Arrogant bastard, he knew it, too.

She swallowed hard, not liking to back down. "Excuse me. I stand corrected," she said, biting the words out grudgingly. "If I've seen enough for today, perhaps we should head back and you can tell me about castrating and tagging and record keeping."

It was just a matter of time, he thought as they turned toward the house. She was getting a feel for how complex and demanding the work was. She wouldn't last long.

They rode in silence despite Kalli's request, riding the horses hard until the last couple of miles when they slowed them to a walk to cool them. By the time they reached the ranch house, Kalli was wilted. She was hot, her hair like a blanket on her back. Tired and sore and disheartened, she wished she could ignore the list of decisions Trace had enumerated. There was more to running this ranch than she thought. And being around Trace was driving her crazy. She'd never wanted anyone to approve of her as she did him. Never wanted anyone to be attracted to her as she did him.

First thing she should do is find a foreman who wanted to run the ranch and let her sit on the porch and sip tea. But until then, she needed Trace. She didn't even know how to go about hiring another foreman. She wished she could treat him as casually as her brothers. But the feelings swamping her weren't in the slightest sisterly.

As they drew up to the barn, Trace stopped by the corral. Easily dismounting, he flung the reins casually over the top rail and walked up to Kalli. She sat on the horse, too tired to even dismount.

Reaching up for her, he clasped his hands lightly around her waist. "Come on, Boss Lady. Get down and go in the house and fix us something cold to drink. A sandwich wouldn't come amiss, either." Gently he drew her from the horse, sliding her to the ground before him. He gazed into her eyes as Kalli gripped his shoulders to steady herself.

Her legs felt like wet spaghetti. Her senses roared out of control with his touch at her waist, with his hard body pressed against hers. His heat engulfed her, and she could smell the faint hint of masculine sweat mixed in with the dust from the corral and hay from the barn. Her hands tightened against the hard muscles of his shoulders, feeling them contract as he drew her even closer.

"You're a tiny thing for a woman full grown," he said huskily.

Kalli pressed against him, relishing the heat that spread from her belly to each extremity. Looking up, she was lost. Tilting her head, she slowly closed her eyes as his face blotted out the sun, coming closer, closer. She moved her lips against his and opened to him when he sought more. His tongue plunged inside the hot cavern of her mouth, learning every bit of her, tracing her teeth, the roof of her mouth, mating with her tongue, inviting it into his mouth.

Kalli was swept away with a riot of sensations she'd never felt before. She was instantly hot, wanting him with a fervor that went beyond anything. She plastered herself against him, feeling her breasts swell with desire, feeling her hands clutching his shoulders with an intensity that shocked her. When his arms came around her and molded her to his long length, she gave a sweet sigh of surrender and moved to deepen their kiss. She was raging out of control and didn't care. It was glorious. The sensations that coursed through her insisted that she comply with the demands of his body.

He swept off her hat and fisted his hand in the thick waves that hung down her back. Her hair was like silk. His other hand skimmed across her rounded bottom, pressing her up and into the hardness that pressed against her belly. She was soft and sweet and hot.

This was madness, but Kalli didn't care. She only wanted to go on forever in Trace's embrace. The world spun out of sight, and there were only the two of them in a creation of their own. A hot, wild, world where his touch awoke needs in her that couldn't be extinguished.

The spell was shattered when her horse bumped them. Staggering slightly, Trace caught her up and turned around so his back was to the mare. Easing away from

Kalli, he stared into her sparkling eyes, his own blank and shuttered. Hell, he hadn't wanted that.

She licked her lips, still tasting him. Smiling tremulously, she cocked her head slightly, feeling bereft as his arms released her and he slowly stood to his full height.

"I thought you didn't like me," she said naively.

"Lady, if you left right now I wouldn't shed a tear. But my damned body wants yours like hell!" He scooped up her hat and set it hard on her head.

Kalli's breathing caught, then released. Her heart pounded at his words, at his kiss. Her fingers longed to run themselves over the heat of his skin, learn the landscape of his muscles, learn what he liked and what he didn't. Her gaze dropped to his lips. She longed for him to kiss her again. Once again she traced her own, tasting him, feeling a shock at the intimacy they'd shared. She blinked again and turned toward the house, her legs shaky and trembling. She needed a respite from him. She couldn't believe she'd kissed him so thoroughly. For heaven's sake, she'd only met him yesterday afternoon. She hadn't even known him a day! Yet she had been attracted to him from the first. If he had pulled her down and tumbled her in the hay, she'd have been willing.

She needed to get control of her hormones. That's what it was. She was so excited to be in Wyoming, she was losing what sense she had. Stepping into the cool kitchen, she tossed her hat on the table and ran her trembling fingers through her hair. She just needed some time to herself to put things into perspective.

He didn't even like her! Yet he wanted her. What kind of relationship would that bring? Ha, that was no relationship, that was sex, pure and simple. Or hot and complex, but sex nonetheless. And she didn't want it. Well, she did, but with more than just animal lust behind it. She wanted caring and love.

Love? From that arrogant, brash cowboy who ordered her around when he was supposed to be working for her? All the time trying to get her ranch? Ha!

She opened the refrigerator and stared sightlessly at it until the cool air brought her around. Slamming it shut, she opened the freezer and took out the frozen lemonade. She hadn't finished unpacking, still needed to get more groceries. She had a million things to do and no time to be mooning around about Trace Longford.

Hunting for a pitcher, she slammed one cupboard door after another in frustration. What good did it do to inherit a ranch lock, stock and barrel if there was nothing to make lemonade with? Finally she drew out a large mixing bowl. It would have to do.

She was measuring the water when she heard his boots on the back steps, and a moment later the screen door slammed behind him. Suddenly the air seemed to arc with tension. Watching the water fill the can, she was afraid to look around. She still had to face him. And not only now, but for days and weeks to come. Her heart began pounding.

She heard a whooshing sound but didn't turn around as his hat sailed onto the table beside hers. Her eyes remained on the lemonade. In two seconds he was beside her, casually leaning one hip against the counter, his arms folded across his chest, his legs crossed as he watched her stir the beverage.

She could see him from the corner of her eye, but refused to meet his gaze. Glad her dark coloring would hide the heat rising in her body, she gave every aspect of concentration to making the lemonade.

"You going to stir that all day?" he asked, amusement lacing his tone.

"If I want to, I will. I'm the boss—"

He broke into her speech by lifting her chin with his warm fingers, tilting her face to meet his.

"It was only a kiss, Kalli. Lighten up. You've been kissed before."

"But not like that," she murmured. Then closed her eyes in anguish. She hadn't wanted to admit it.

When his thumb brushed across her mouth, her eyes flew open.

"You can't stay here, Kalli. It's too much for you. You don't know enough and aren't going to have enough time to learn it before you run the place into the ground. Give it up and go home." His gaze was on her mouth, on the movement of his thumb across her lips.

"This is my home," she said breathlessly. "I'll learn all I need to know to run the place. And in the meantime I can hire people who do know."

"While you stay—" he ignored her vow to remain "—I'll help you out. And if you want more than a few chaste kisses, I'm willing. I want you, Kalli."

God, she didn't know how to deal with such blatant desire. The men she'd dated in Boston had been smooth, sophisticated, restrained. They would never have been so blunt, especially on such short acquaintance.

But none of them had ever stirred her senses as Trace did. She took a deep breath and clasped his wrist with her hand, longing to push him away, yet clamoring for more of his touch. Idly she noted his pulse was strong and steady, not racing like hers. His eyes met hers and he gazed at her for a long moment. She felt as if he could see into her soul.

"Please, Trace. I can't. I don't know you. You don't know me. It's too soon." She knew she wasn't doing a good job of it, but she could scarcely think with the blood thrumming through her veins, the heat of his hand scorching her.

He let his gaze slip across her, stalling for time while he tried to think. Her breasts were high and firm, a little on the small side. Yet his palms itched to cup them, feel their weight, make her nipples harden against his hot skin. Her waist was narrow, her hips gently flared, filling the jeans she wore like a man's dream. Being with her fostered a hunger in him he hadn't felt in a long, long time. He didn't like it any more than she did.

Hell.

"So you call the shots, Boss Lady. Are you going to serve up that lemonade?" He moved away, sat at the table, his legs sprawled out before him, his thumbs tucked into his empty belt loops as he watched her.

"Yes." She turned, glad of the activity. She would call the shots. She was the boss and she had better remember that. She was used to advising patients what to do. Maybe she could pretend Trace was a patient. Would he mind? Somehow she thought of him more as the recalcitrant kind, challenging her every recommendation, then doing whatever he damned well pleased.

She set the two glasses on the table and pulled out a chair, as far from him as she could get.

"I'm hungry," he said after he pulled a long drink from the glass.

She frowned. "I'm not your cook."

He shrugged and stood, reaching for his hat.

"I'll be back tomorrow then. See you."

"Wait! Trace, where are you going?"

"I'm hungry. If you're not going to feed me, I'll go home for lunch. Need to check on Becky anyway. But it's too long a drive to come back today and get anything done. I'll be back tomorrow."

"Dammit, I'll fix you lunch!" She jumped up and crossed angrily to the refrigerator. He was pushing his luck. Just wait until she knew something about ranching. She'd tell him to take a flying leap. She hadn't come all the way from Boston to end up with some arrogant cowboy who thought she should wait on him hand and foot. Dammit, she was the boss—not him.

"Mind if I use your phone while you fix it?" he asked, amusement dancing in his dark eyes.

"No." She knew she was overreacting, but she was so mad she could spit. All she wanted to do was come out here and enjoy her ranch. Now she had a hot-blooded cowboy disturbing her beyond belief. One that didn't even like her and was constantly pointing out her short-comings as far as ranching was concerned. All he wanted was her ranch, and she was catering to all his needs. First breakfast, now lunch. Did he expect dinner, too?

For a moment she was distracted. Dinner. Quiet, with candles and maybe even a fire in the fireplace. It got cool here in the mountains at night. Even in May. After a nice meal, veal perhaps, or beef, they'd sip their wine, talk quietly. He'd kiss her again. Run his hands over her—

"Ow!" She'd sliced her finger. No more daydreaming. Or if she did any, it had to be about the ranch, not some sexy cowboy.

She set their places as Trace came back.

"Your daughter okay?" she asked.

"Fine."

"And your ranch doesn't need you while you're here?" she asked as she began eating the luncheon-meat sandwich. She wished she'd had some real ham or roast beef. She needed to get to the store.

Trace looked up, hesitated a moment. "I've got a good foreman."

"Maybe you should run your own place and send him over here."

"I prefer this setup."

"I bet. Anytime you see me doing anything wrong, you can jump in with another offer to buy me out."

"Maybe." He ate the light lunch, pleased with the hearty helpings she'd dished up.

"You sure are talkative when you want to tell me what I can't do and everything I don't know. But trying to get you to tell me anything about yourself dries you up faster than an antihistamine."

He blinked at her analogy and smiled. "What do you want to know, Kalli? I've told you the important stuff. I'm not married so an affair between us will hurt no one. I don't think you can make it on the ranch. Now, before you get all puffed up and addled, let me say it won't be for lack of trying. But it's just too much unless you've been born and bred to it. Philip was having a tough time, and he'd been doing it for years."

"A lot of ranchers are very successful," she protested.

"Yeah, and a lot go broke. Stay for a few days and learn all you can, but then look at it long and hard. I think you should accept my offer."

He flicked her a glance, wondering when she would order him off the property. As soon as she could get a competent manager, he guessed. He had to make sure no one tried for the job. He had a vested interest in seeing the place managed properly. He didn't want the thing falling apart before he took over. It might take a little while to get rid of her, but she wouldn't stay. He knew all about city girls enamored with thoughts of ranches and cowboys, but the reality was too stark. Too far from parties and shops and good times, they had to leave. He could wait her out.

Kalli nibbled on her sandwich as thoughts spun and tumbled around in her mind. She was extremely conscious of Trace sitting a few feet from her. Wondering how long she could maintain this heightened sense of awareness, she remembered his words earlier. *I want you.*

"—computers?" he asked.

She blinked and stared at him. "What?"

"I said, do you know much about computers?" He looked at her. What had she been thinking about?

"A little. At the hospital we did all our records on them. Why?"

"All the ranch records are on a computer. Philip put one in about four years ago. We can review the programs and you can get started in bringing your records up to date this afternoon. I'll get you started, then I really do have to head for home."

She nodded, torn between wanting him to stay and the relief she knew she'd feel when he was gone. She needed time to get herself back on track. Decide exactly what she was going to do about him. She couldn't believe she was reacting so strongly, just because he was the sexiest thing she'd ever seen.

"Let's get started. Don't want to hold you up from leaving," she said, jumping up and walking quickly from the room to the office she'd discovered on her explorations last night.

He was right behind her, and when she sank down in the chair behind the desk, he sat on the arm, his hip pressing against her, his body leaning over hers as he reached across to flick on the machine.

Staring at the monitor as if it was a talisman, Kalli refused to give in to the urge to lean against him, to tilt her head back for a kiss and forget records and computers and the ranch. Instead, she listened as attentively as she could as he explained how to boot up and get into the program and how to select the different options for input and report generation.

"I've got it," she said impatiently when he reviewed it all a second time. "How much stuff has to be put into it before it's up to date?"

"Several months. I tried to keep up with it, but with my own, it was just too much. Here are the receipts, payroll records, calving notes and bills yet to be paid. You can make a start. When you have everything in, let me know and we'll run some quick reports to make sure it's in right, then run a full set of records."

"I can manage," she said, counting the minutes until he left. Until she could breathe normally, regain her customary heart rate and relax her tight control.

"Yeah, I bet. See you tomorrow, then, Kalli." He rose and started across the room.

"Trace?"

"Yeah?" He paused in the doorway and looked back.

"If I need to get you before you come over tomorrow, how do I call you?"

"I'll give you my phone number. You can reach me if I'm not here, or leave a message." He walked to the desk and scrawled his phone number on a piece of paper.

"I won't call unless it's important, of course. I wouldn't want you to think I can't make it here," she said, tucking the paper safely into the top drawer.

He smiled, "Yeah, right." He traced a knuckle down her cheek and nodded, leaving the room with the same graceful, liquid prowl she'd seen yesterday. God, he was sexy!

Three

Determined to prove to Trace that she was capable of running a ranch, that she was not some innocent city woman who had come to be pampered, Kalli set her alarm for five the next morning. She'd be up, dressed and have breakfast ready when he arrived at six. She wasn't afraid of hard work. Nursing was often hard. The frantic pace of the emergency room left little time for taking things easy. If he thought she was used to just sitting around, she'd prove to him she could pull her own weight.

All good intentions aside, she hadn't figured on being so sore and stiff! With a groan she rolled over and slammed her hand down on the alarm knob. Every inch of her body ached. She hurt in muscles she hadn't even known about, despite the anatomy courses in college. Sleep had been elusive during the night as she had tossed and turned and tried to get comfortable after her warm bath. Nothing worked.

And it wasn't only her aching body that had kept sleep at bay. Her thoughts had revolved around Trace. How adamant he was about her not being able to stay. How he had looked sitting on a horse. How exciting his body had felt against hers when he'd kissed her by the corral. The last led to fantasies about future kisses, and that in turn led to erotic dreams of more than kissing when she did manage to sleep fitfully. All in all, a restless and uncomfortable night.

Now it was five o'clock and he would be here in an hour and she wanted nothing so much as to roll over and sleep for another ten hours.

Slowly she dragged herself out of bed. A quick shower revived her enough to get dressed. Knowing how hot the day would be, she braided her hair for coolness. Maybe she should get it cut, but its warmth would be welcomed in the cold winter months of Wyoming. And she rather liked it long.

She'd think on it.

Slowly she made her way to the kitchen. The first faint traces of dawn glimmered. The sky was lighter in the east, the faint outlines of the mountains barely discernible in the west. She measured coffee, started the machine and turned to get some eggs. She had to go shopping today. The few things she'd picked up on her way here had only been to tide her over, to give her a chance to scope out what the ranch held and make a list of all she needed. The light shopping she'd done certainly hadn't been enough to provide for Trace's hearty appetite, as well.

She should have made her list yesterday, or last night. But she had stayed at the computer until she was bleary-eyed and much too tired to think, much less plan meals and make a list of groceries. She'd have to make time today. Both to make the list and purchase the food.

Right at six she heard the truck pull in and the engine cut off. Satisfied, she dished up the eggs and sausages and stacked the toast on another plate.

"Good morning!" she said brightly as he walked in, pleased as punch at the look of disbelief on his face. It made all the effort worthwhile.

"Morning. You been up all night?" he asked as he tossed his hat on the rack and sat on the chair he'd used yesterday.

"No, just got up a little while ago. Dig in. We've lots to do today." She eased herself down in the chair and prayed the day's activities didn't include riding. Even the seat of the chair was uncomfortable.

She watched him as he served himself from the platter, amazed at the strong pull of attraction she felt so early in the morning. Every inch ached, and all she could think was that one of his kisses would make everything better.

Oh, great. She groaned internally. Was today to be a repeat of yesterday? Was she going to have to watch her every thought to make sure she didn't just throw herself against him and ask him to make love to her?

"How far did you get with the records?" he asked.

"Part way through February. There's a lot of stuff." Thank God he didn't suspect the wayward tendencies of her thoughts. She had to concentrate on ranch business.

"Yeah. Philip was sick for a long time before I realized how bad things were. A lot of things slid. Then at the end, he couldn't do anything. He was behind when I stepped in and I never caught up."

"Well, a few more marathon sessions like yesterday and I'll be caught up," she said with quiet confidence. Once she got the hang of everything, the organization had gone fast. But there was a lot of information still to input into the computer. And she didn't have a clue what she was going to do with all the information once she was finished. Maybe Trace would explain what she was to look for.

"Thought today we'd ride out with José and Tim. You can get to know them, see how they work. We can check the fences and water holes at the same time. Give you a better feel for your land," Trace said easily. He glanced up in time to catch the grimace that crossed her face.

"Problem with that?" he asked silkily. Was she still wanting to give orders? Was she going to fight his every suggestion?

"No. No problem with that." She swallowed hard and thought about the aspirin and Motrin she'd need to take before they left. At least she'd be numb for part of the day. What would they say if she asked for a pillow for her saddle?

"I'll let the men know. We'll leave in fifteen minutes. Can you be ready by then?"

"Of course."

He smiled sardonically, knowing she'd never admit to any kind of weakness. He'd seen the careful way she was walking, sitting. She was feisty, his Kalli.

His Kalli? Hell. He snatched his hat and stormed from the kitchen. She wasn't his. And he didn't want her, except maybe for a roll in the hay. She would be leaving soon, he'd make damn sure of that.

Kalli scraped the dishes and soaked them in a sink full of water. She took the aspirin and grabbed her hat. Slowly walking to the barn, she tried to loosen her muscles. Maybe a longer soak in the tub last night would have helped. She'd been so smug about her riding yesterday. But it was obvious now that a couple of hours a week of riding in Boston had not prepared her for endless hours each day on a horse in Wyoming. She took a deep breath. She would not let these men know how much she hated riding with them today. She'd keep up with them if it was the last thing she did! There was no way she'd give Trace an opening to comment on her unsuitability, much as he might enjoy it.

José and Tim had their horses saddled and Trace was just finishing with hers. She smiled at the men, struck by the odd atmosphere. The two cowboys appeared almost awkward. They tipped their hats and greeted her quietly, sending a sidelong glance to Trace. He ignored them, tightening the cinch and flipping the stirrup down.

"Need a hand?" he asked as Kalli stepped up beside the sorrel gelding.

The first thing she was going to do when she was more comfortable with being in charge was get a mounting block. Trace wouldn't be here every time she wanted to ride. She had to be self-sufficient. Though she wondered how she'd ever manage to toss the heavy saddle on a horse as high as this one.

"Please."

Trace watched her reach up for the saddle horn and took her foot when she stepped into his laced hands. Her hand burned into his shoulder as she steadied herself, holding on as if for dear life. For a long moment, time was suspended as she hovered between earth and horse, between today and yesterday. He found himself staring into her dark eyes. When his gaze dropped to her mouth, he remembered the sweet taste. He saw her draw a deep breath and hesitate. Flicking a quick glance to the others, he was relieved to see they were talking and not watching Kalli mount.

"Get on the horse, Kalli," he said in a low, hoarse whisper.

She scrambled for her seat, the heat that flooded her erasing the aches and pains of her sore muscles. She settled her hat in an effort to cover up the embarrassment she felt at Trace's knowing look. A quick glance at José and Tim assured her they had noticed nothing. Mounted and ready to ride, they sat easily in their saddles, talking quietly.

The quartet moved out of the barn and to the east, picking up the pace as soon as they cleared the yard. Kalli clenched her teeth to keep back the groan she longed to give voice to. She could only hope that exercise would be the way to loosen the muscles and ease the pain.

No one spoke as the horses loped across the early morning dew. The grass was green and lush, the sky a clear, deep blue, and behind them the granite spires of the Tetons shone like sparkling diamonds in the sun's rays. Kalli looked around her in delight. It was a perfect day and she was on her own ranch. Did life get any better?

By late morning they had ridden the perimeter of two large sections, surveying all the fencing, getting a rough count of the cattle grazing, checking the watering holes, the ponds and the Snake River, which touched the property in a couple of places. These sources gave unlimited water to her cattle. The banks were checked for winter damage, but found to be sound.

Kalli rode for a while with José and found out that, despite his Spanish name, he was third-generation Wyomingite and never had any desire to see the rest of the world. Mid-morning she traded places with Trace and partnered Tim. He was from California, had grown up on cattle ranches and then followed the rodeo circuit. When she found that out, she questioned him excitedly. He answered her questions with a laugh, amused by her avid interest, drawing the conversation to a close saying, ''Well, ma'am, almost every cowboy does a rodeo or two. Only the really good ones make any money at it. Like Trace.''

''Trace did rodeos?'' She looked ahead where he and José discussed a section of fencing that needed repair. She could envision him riding some wild horse or bull.

"Rode, ma'am. Trace rode the rodeos. And did damn well at it. He made big money before he quit. That's how he—" Tim closed his mouth and looked at Trace.

"How he what?"

He urged his horse faster, catching up with the two other men.

"How he what?" Kalli repeated as she drew even with them, her eyes involuntarily going to Trace, even though she was still waiting for Tim's reply.

"Trace, I was telling Kalli how you used to ride the rodeos," Tim said, almost desperately.

Trace nodded, his eyes studying Kalli.

"You didn't tell me," she said, holding his gaze.

"Never came up."

"Tim wouldn't tell me the rest," she said, her curiosity rampant.

"That's how I made my living when I was younger. But it's a sport for the young. These old bones wouldn't stand for it now."

She grinned. "Why, Trace, you don't look a day over forty." That ought to pay him back some for saying she wasn't up to ranching.

"Forty! Hell, woman, I'm only thirty-four!"

She laughed. "Excuse me. I thought you said you were old."

"Too old for rodeoing. Are you here to learn about ranching or to insult me?"

She caught her lower lip between her teeth, laughter still shimmering in her eyes. "Learn, oh wise elder." She giggled softly, daring him to ignore the humor.

The soft lights in his eyes gave him away. But he turned to José and began laying out plans for replacing the sections of fencing.

Kalli listened with half an ear, wondering why Tim had looked so worried. Was there more to Trace's riding the rodeo than they wanted her to know? She was intrigued.

What other aspects of her foreman should she be aware of? Or were they wondering if she knew who he was? That he was the one offering to buy her out?

She wished she could have seen him at a rodeo, all cocky and arrogant, strutting around like the cowboys she'd seen. She'd only been to a couple of rodeos in her life and had found them fascinating. She would make sure she went to any held in the area.

"Daydreaming again, Boss Lady?" Trace asked as he pushed his horse against hers, his hard thigh brushing hers.

She looked up. José and Tim were already several dozen yards across the section, heading up a steep incline. Trace was watching her with those dark eyes, his look holding hers.

"I was thinking about rodeos," she admitted reluctantly. "Are there any around here?"

"Will be later on. Jackson has a big one. If you're still here, I'll take you."

"If I'm still here? Oh, I assure you, Trace Longford, I'll still be here whenever it comes to town." She tilted her chin and kicked the side of her horse, moving to catch up to José and Tim before Trace could stop her. How like him to tell her she'd go with him. Maybe she'd find another date. Or maybe . . . Maybe she would go with him. Her heart sped up a little at the thought. Who better to escort her than someone who knew all about rodeos?

It was early afternoon by the time they returned to the homestead. Kalli was so tired and sore she could scarcely stay in the saddle. Yet every time she felt Trace's eyes on her, she made an effort to sit up and look at ease. She wouldn't admit to any weakness before him. He already didn't think she'd make the grade. She refused to give him any ammunition to strengthen that belief.

But when they pulled up by the corral she looked longingly at her house. Would it be possible to ride the horse up to her bedroom window, flip open the screen and fall directly into bed? She wasn't sure she could walk the distance. She hurt!

Trace, José and Tim quickly dismounted, tying their horses to the rail and loosening the cinches. Trace slapped his mount on the rump and walked over to her, eyeing her suspiciously.

"Going to stay on the horse all day?"

"I thought I would," she said, slumping a little.

"Tired?" He rested his hand on her thigh.

Kalli felt it like a brand. She stared at his tanned skin, the long fingers, the strong wrist. The heat from his palm seared her. She flicked a look into his eyes and thought she detected a glimpse of sympathy.

"Actually, I thought I'd ride over and get a better look at the mountains. Maybe see how high the horse could climb—"

She gave a shout as he reached up and pulled her down.

"Trace!" She sagged against him, her legs like rubber. He held her easily, turning to call to Tim.

"Come get her horse and turn him loose. She's not riding any more today." He leaned over a bit and swept her up into his arms.

"Trace, put me down." But her arms encircled his neck and she held on for dear life. Fighting the urge to lay her head against his shoulder and close her eyes, she glared at him instead as he marched determinedly across the yard toward the back door.

"Thought you said you'd been riding since you learned about inheriting the ranch," he said.

She was impressed he could carry her so easily, talk in a normal tone and not be out of breath. "I did. But only a couple of hours a week. In a ring. How do you do it day after day?"

"Practice. We've been riding since we were kids. And this is an easy day. Sometimes during roundup or bad weather, we're twelve, eighteen hours in the saddle." He opened the screen door and set her on her feet. "Can you manage a bath and then bed, Boss Lady?" he asked, his hands still on her shoulders, giving her support.

"Let's get one thing straight here, Trace. My name is Kalli. Calling me Boss Lady won't cut it. We both know I haven't called a single shot since I arrived here. 'Fix me something to eat, let's go riding, go do the accounts!' You're the real boss of the Triple T, and until I learn lots more I guess it's going to stay that way."

He smiled into her glaring eyes. "Yeah, I guess it is."

His eyes warmed and the rough planes of his face softened just a little with the smile. And Kalli lost her train of thought. He was the sexiest thing she'd ever seen, and her heart began pumping hot blood through her veins. She stared, mesmerized, longing for more, knowing he had to get back to work. Knowing she was probably no more than an amusing incident to him. But it didn't matter. Her gaze dropped to his lips and her body shivered traitorously. She wanted—

As if he could read her mind, his mouth covered hers in a hot kiss. His lips moved persuasively over hers until she opened at his silent command and welcomed him. His tongue slipped in, tracing her teeth, moving beyond to tease then dance with her tongue.

Blood roared in her ears, and her breathing became labored. Kalli pressed closer, feeling weak and feminine and invincible and desirable. Her hands gripped his arms, holding on lest she float away in a cloud of sweet delight.

He pulled back and stared at her, gently wiping her lips with his thumb, the hard calluses lending an erotic roughness to his touch. Again he traced her lower lip, his thumb exquisitely gentle.

"Soak your muscles and then take a nap. You'll feel better in a day or two. In the meantime, get to work on those accounts," he ordered.

"Yes, sir, boss," she whispered, her eyes clinging to his.

"Hell, Kalli, don't look at me like that unless you want to start more than I think you do."

She remembered he'd told her he wanted her. It would be unfair to continue if she wasn't ready to take the next step. And she wasn't. She'd just met the man. It didn't matter that he attracted her more than anyone she'd ever met before. It didn't matter that she felt special beyond imagination when she was with him. It *did* matter, however, that he didn't seem to like her much. With a soft sigh, she pulled back and tried a small smile.

"Thank you for seeing me home," she said in a throaty whisper. She turned and limped toward the bathroom, refusing to let her mind dwell on the possibility of the two of them in bed together.

But her body remembered his touch, and tingled.

Kalli soaked in the tub until she was as wrinkled as a prune. Slipping on a long T-shirt she'd swiped from her brother Tony, she lay across her bed facedown. Her bottom was so sore it hurt to lie on her back. Closing her eyes, she relaxed her tired, aching muscles. It felt so good. There was so much to do, she'd just rest for a few minutes. But it felt so good. . . .

It was dark when Kalli awoke. She lay in the peaceful evening, almost too lethargic to rise. Her stomach grumbled, letting her know she hadn't had anything to eat since breakfast. Slowly she pushed herself up and padded barefoot into the kitchen. She ate a quick sandwich standing at the counter, making her grocery list as she ate. At least the day wouldn't be a total waste, though she absolutely had to go get groceries tomorrow or end up eating with the men. Which wouldn't be all bad, unless Trace was there to undermine her authority before them. She frowned. He wouldn't do such a thing. He'd never hinted at anything before the men. But just instructing her on the way to run the ranch could undermine the men's confidence in her. They'd do better to continue to eat apart.

Finishing that task, she wandered into the office. Sitting gingerly on the chair, she put the March bills and payments in chronological order. Restless, she pushed them away. She wasn't up to working on the computer tonight. She hunted up her boxes of books and rummaged around until she found a favorite Louis L'Amour. Taking it to bed, she propped herself up and began to read.

When the alarm rang the next morning, Kalli shut it off and lay back in bed. God, she did not want to get up! She was stiff as a board and every movement spiked pain into her muscles. How did Trace and José and Tim do it day after day? Even with practice, she couldn't imagine becoming used to riding for hours at a time.

Slowly she stretched, forcing her muscles to respond. Sitting on the side of the bed, she wondered if she should just throw in the towel.

The phone rang. She jumped. The ring was loud in the silence of early dawn.

"Hello?"

"Kalli? It's Trace."

"Is something wrong?" She turned to look out the window. It was still dark, but dawn was only minutes away.

"Yeah, problem here. I was up all night and I'm just dead on my feet. I can't come by this morning."

"What's wrong? Do you need my help?"

"No, had a mare in foal, there were problems, complications. The vet's been here all night, too. Anyway, it's all over now. We have a nice filly and the mare's doing fine. But I'm beat."

"Yeah, you're too old for all-nighters like that," she said softly, lying back against her pillows.

"Yeah."

She could hear his chuckle across the line.

"You up?"

"My alarm just went off. I'm still in bed."

"How do you feel today?"

"Older than you."

"Hell, maybe we both need a day in bed."

Together? Kalli smiled dreamily at the thought.

"Yeah, maybe. Any orders for the day, boss?" she asked.

"Catch up on the accounts. You can sit on a pillow in a chair."

"When do I get a day off?"

"You just got here." *Just got here,* he thought. He felt as if he'd been thinking about her all his life. Had it only been three days? He had it bad. He needed to get her out of his system and go back to ranching. She had to sell her place soon, or he'd go crazy.

"Trace?"

"Yeah?"

"Want to come to dinner? After all, I'm so used to cooking for two now that I'm sure I'll make too much for just me." She held her breath.

"I usually eat dinner with Becky," he said.

"Good, bring her, too. I'd like to meet her," she said quickly before he could refuse.

"All right. We'll be over around six."

"See you then."

She hung up the phone and lay back, her smile almost gleeful. Resetting her alarm for a more reasonable hour, Kalli blissfully fell asleep.

She drove into Jackson later that morning. First stop was the attorney who had handled her uncle's will. He had mentioned bank accounts and statements the day she'd met him. But now she wanted to get everything cleared and established so she could write checks.

Richard Strominger happened to be free when she arrived unannounced, and he saw her right away.

"How are things going, Miss Bonotelli?" He was an older man, easygoing and relaxed. His casual Western attire added to her concept of the Old West aspect still prevalent in Wyoming. She grinned as she shook his hand and sat in the chair opposite his desk.

"Great. The Triple T's the most wonderful place. I'm so pleased with the way everything is going," she replied.

"Still planning to stay?" He watched her over steepled fingers.

She nodded, wondering why every male out here thought she shouldn't. Was it some sort of Western macho thing?

"You've got a good offer from the Flying Cloud Ranch. Wouldn't you like to at least consider it? I don't know how long it will stay open," Richard advised her.

"No. I've already told Trace my answer. I'm not selling. I'm learning all I can to run the place myself," she said.

"I see. Very well, I'll send a formal refusal."

She signed the necessary papers to complete the transfer of all titles into her name. Then Richard personally walked her over to the bank, introduced her to the bank president and helped smooth the transition there.

"Glad to have you as a client. Triple T's been with us since the beginning. Though I heard there was an offer to buy you out by Flying Cloud," the bank president said as they sat waiting for her new checks to be printed.

"I'm not selling," she said quietly. Was this the small-town grapevine at work? Somehow she didn't think Richard Strominger would be telling everyone his clients' business. And she certainly couldn't picture Trace doing so.

"I see. Well, good. It's our gain." He smiled genially and asked her about Boston.

Kalli was struck by the friendliness of everyone she met. Even at the supermarket, the cashier and clerk had been welcoming, though they, too, had mentioned Trace's offer. Kalli shook her head, amazed. Would everyone in town now be commiserating with him on the lost sale? He'd love that. Shaking her head again, she forgot about it as she hurried home. With any luck she'd have a chance for another soak to ease her aching muscles.

Happy that Trace and his daughter were coming for dinner, she prepared veal scallopini. It was her mother's special recipe and she hoped they liked it. For a moment she hesitated. Would they like Italian food? Nonsense, everyone did.

While Kalli loved the West and dressing like a cowboy, she decided to dress up a little for the first dinner guests in her new home. She donned a dusky rose skirt with a matching scooped-neck top that buttoned down the front, then French braided her hair to keep it neat. She didn't want to be worried about it while she cooked. She used a light touch of makeup and sprayed perfume on sparingly.

When Trace drove into the yard, she was ready. A final check of the table revealed everything set perfectly. She wished she could have used the dining room, but the kitchen would have to do. She didn't want to make too big a deal over dinner.

Trace walked in as if he owned the place. His daughter followed, peering around her tall father to stare at Kalli.

"Hello. Welcome. Are you Becky? I'm Kalli." She offered her hand to the girl, who was as tall as she. When

Becky was full grown, she'd probably be as tall as her daddy, and for certain taller than Kalli. With a silent sigh, Kalli reflected it didn't take much to be taller than her.

"Hello." Becky shook her hand then stepped back, looking boldly around her. She met Kalli's eyes again and studied her for a long minute.

"Are you part Indian, too?" she asked.

"No, are you?" Kalli replied, surprised by the girl's question.

Becky nodded and looked at her father. Trace had put his hat on the rack and turned to face them. His eyes became watchful and his stance wary.

"We're part Shoshone," he said.

"Well, I'm full Italian, though my family has been over here for three generations. Not a long time in comparison to yours, I guess," Kalli said easily, smiling at them both. She had wondered if he was part Indian.

"Dinner is just about ready. Do you want to eat and then move to the living room? Do you think it's cool enough for a fire?"

Trace nodded, motioning to Becky to take a chair, holding it for her. He moved behind Kalli's chair as she brought the platters to the table. He seated her, then took the chair he normally used.

Serving the plates, Kalli made sure her guests had everything they needed. Becky watched her warily the entire time. Kalli wondered if it was because there was no woman at their place and Becky was curious. Or was there something more?

Conversation was stilted, awkward, erratic. Father and daughter ate steadily, apparently unconcerned at the silence.

"So," Kalli said brightly when she could no longer stand the silence. "Tell me all about the new mother and baby. What are you going to name it?"

Trace nodded to Becky to answer.

"We're calling her Cloud's Pride. My dad owns the Flying Cloud Ranch," Becky said with arrogant pride. "And before long he says he'll own this one, too."

Four

Kalli stared at Trace, feeling as if one of the horses in the corral had kicked her in the stomach. Was she never to escape his claim? Was he bragging about it to his daughter? Every chance he had, he told her she'd never make it, undermining any confidence she felt in her ability to run her ranch, constantly urging her to accept the buy-out offer. And why not? He coveted her ranch.

Trace remained silent, his dark eyes watching her, his lips pressed tightly together. Becky stared wide-eyed between the two adults, her expression unsure and worried.

"You have some nerve bragging to your daughter that you're getting this place. I'm tired of you telling me I don't belong here—"

"You don't belong here," he interrupted. "You're some starry-eyed romantic city girl who thinks the wild West is alive and waiting to fulfill your fantasies. That living on a ranch would be the same thing as visiting it when you were a kid. Sweetheart, as soon as the novelty wears off, you'll leave so fast it'll make your head spin. I'm just trying to keep you from running the place into the ground before you take off."

"And the kisses, were they to try to seduce me out of the ranch?" A tearing pain pierced her. Had his kisses only been a way to manipulate her? Try to get her to agree to sell? She'd almost relaxed her guard around him. It had been a mistake.

He flicked a glance at Becky. "Go see Josh," he ordered.

"I want to stay here." She pouted.

"Go!"

She frowned but slowly shoved back her chair and pushed away from the table. With a glare at Kalli, the girl stomped out of the room, letting the screen door bang shut behind her. For a few seconds her footsteps in the gravel could be heard and then they faded away.

Trace's eyes never left Kalli. He could see the hurt and anger reflected in her eyes and didn't like it. He hadn't meant to hurt her. But he knew as sure as he was sitting here that she'd never make it. And he'd been up-front with her, he wanted the ranch.

"I'm sorry," Kalli said. "I shouldn't have said that in front of Becky."

"You shouldn't have said it at all."

"Oh, sure, it's fine for you to come in and throw your weight around, but if I say anything I'm wrong." She jumped up and began pacing the room. "You can just get out, Trace. I don't need help like yours. I'll find another foreman." She stopped across the room from him, leaned against the counter and tilted her head, looking far more confident than she really felt.

He rose, all six feet of him, and strode across the wooden floor, the heels of his boots stomping until he stopped mere inches from her, pressing her back against the tile edge. Glaring at her, he shook his head.

"No. You're not getting another foreman. I'll do it until you decide to sell."

"I'm not going to sell!" Kalli almost screamed in frustration. Why wouldn't he listen to her? If he thought he could drive her away, he didn't know her very well. Maybe her family should clue him in. They knew how stubborn and tenacious she could be. They had tried to talk her out of becoming a nurse, citing the physical strain and arguing that the emotional trauma would unravel her. But Kalli had become a nurse. And yes, it had been hard sometimes, but the rewards had been well worth it. As would the reward of making a go of her ranch.

"You're fired," she said. "Get out and don't come back."

He stepped closer, crowding her. She had to tilt her head back until her neck ached, the coolness of the tile like a band across her lower back. He was so tall, so strong and so damned male!

"I'm not leaving," he said, his voice low, threatening. He raised his hand.

"Don't touch me. If you think you can seduce me into agreeing to sell, you're crazy."

He reached out and clasped her waist, tossing her up on the edge of the counter. Pressing open her knees, he stepped between her legs, bunching up her skirt, his hands hard and hot on her waist, clamping her in place even as she wiggled to escape. Lowering his face until his nose almost touched hers, he spoke softly, almost menacingly.

"Let's get one thing straight here, sweetheart. I want you. I told you that before. But it doesn't have a thing in hell to do with getting your ranch. If I sleep with you from now to doomsday, I'll still want the ranch. If you never let me touch you again, I'll still want the ranch, and I'll get it.''

''I don't want you to touch me.'' She had meant to sound assertive, strong. But her voice came out almost wistful.

''Liar. I can see the pulse point in your throat, your heart is racing.''

''From fear,'' she said. Or excitement, or anticipation or fierce yearning. She could feel her heart pounding, the blood roaring hot through her veins.

''Liar,'' he repeated. His gaze dropped to her mouth when she nervously licked her lips. He stared at the moisture for a long moment, then slowly pressed his lips against hers, capturing the wetness on his own. Slowly his tongue traced her lips, moistening them, rubbing along the seam. Not pressing forth, not trying for anything but a taste of her.

Kalli closed her eyes to better enjoy the sensation. His breath fanned across her cheek. His tongue slowly, gently rubbed against her lips. She parted them slightly to allow him access to her mouth, but he held off. Shockingly aware of the intimacy of their position, she leaned into the embrace, her hands inching up his arms to encircle his neck and hold his head so he couldn't pull back.

At the feel of her capitulation, Trace's hands pulled her hard against him, until there was not an inch of space between their bodies. He could feel the heat of her inner core through the straining denim of his jeans. He could feel her soft breath catch and release as she breathed against his cheek. Her pounding heart slammed against his chest as her firm breasts pressed against him. She felt so damned good.

Plunging his tongue into the warm welcome of her mouth, he tightened his grip even more, moving his arms around her, one hand cupping the firm globe of her bottom and hauling her even closer. The other trailed up until it captured the back of her head. Longing to delve his fingers into that dark glossy mane, he began to impatiently undo the elaborate braid that held it.

Warning bells clamored in her mind, but Kalli ignored them. Trace's taste beguiled, lured. Her tongue mated with his, danced with it in enchanting fascination. Every nerve ending clamored for more. Pressing herself into his long body, honed hard as the granite of the distant mountains, stronger than the men she was used to and far more dangerous, she reveled in the sensations flooding her, sweeping through her like the hot prairie wind.

Danger. That was the allure. And the risk. Trace wanted her. He wanted her ranch. When he got both, he'd move on. She'd be out on her ear, tossed aside, discarded. Danger. But it was the danger that bewitched, like a flame for a moth.

Blinking, she pulled away a little. Knowing in her mind she needed to stop, to put some distance between herself and this dangerous cowboy, her body was still reluctant to end the embrace. Even though she wrenched her mouth free, her fingers refused to relinquish their tantalizing foray into the thickness of his hair.

"Trace, stop, please," she whispered, breathing hard. Her breasts ached with desire for more of his touch. The liquid heat within her clamored for the quenching plunge that would first consume her, then release her. Her body wanted his as much as his desired hers. But it was a foolhardy, greedy craving that would only lead to desolation. She had to have more than mere sex.

"You want me, Kalli. I can feel it," he said against her mouth, moving to brush sweet kisses across her cheek, trail down her throat and lick the rapid pulse.

"Sex is not enough," she said regretfully, her fingers still entangled in his hair, her legs loosely looped around his hips. Slowly she pushed him away, tried to scoot back on the counter, aware of his hand on her hip like a brand, hot and possessive.

"What are you looking for, protestations of love?" He allowed her to move away and stood straight, his hands dropping to loosely rest on her spread thighs.

"You don't even like me." Gazing into his eyes was like looking into the midnight of a mountain mist, the gleaming polish of obsidian.

"What's not to like? You are one sexy lady. But you're going to be here for such a short time. Let's not waste it. Dammit, lady, you'll play at ranching until you get bored, or the first setback hits you. Then you'll be back to the bright city lights as fast as a plane can take you. I know your type."

"You don't know me. I'm not a type!"

"The hell you're not. I married a woman like you. I know exactly your type. Can't get enough of a romantic cowboy until the dirt and sweat and monotony of the life disgust and bore you. Then you'll take off to find something more exciting."

She stared at him. Rampant curiosity rose at the mention of his wife. Of the circumstances he'd described. Had she told him that when she left? Or was he just imagining things? Was he trying to rationalize Alyssa's leaving?

Kalli had a million questions. "She was a city girl?"

"From Denver. Hooked on rodeo cowboys. Life was just dandy as long as we followed the circuit, but too dull and boring when we came back to the ranch to settle down, try to make a go of things. She craved the excitement of the rodeo, and the cowboy of choice didn't matter much, as long as he was part of the action."

"Were you hurt when she left?" Kalli asked, stunned at the bitterness of his tone. Of course he'd been hurt. The woman he'd loved had left him.

"I had a year-old baby to take care of. I didn't have time to be hurt, only mad as hell." He leaned his hands against the edge of the counter, leaning over her as if to prevent her from ever moving. He no longer touched, yet Kalli felt every movement, every breath he took. The tension rose even higher.

"To love someone and then—"

"God, but you view the world from rose-colored glasses. There was no love between us. Alyssa was great in the sack. She got pregnant with Becky so I married her to give my kid a name. There was no love there. On either side. Grow up, Kalli, people mate for various reasons, and the romantic love you're talking about is only found in fairy tales."

"You're so cynical. Love is all around you. Don't you love Becky?"

"Of course, she's my daughter."

"Well, there's other love, too. And nothing is stronger than the love between a man and a woman. It can last beyond the grave. Just because you haven't experienced it doesn't mean it doesn't exist," she snapped. Where had all the anger come from? He'd been fair with her, telling her exactly what he wanted—her, the ranch. The anger couldn't be on his behalf, could it?

"And you have firsthand knowledge, I suppose." For a moment he held his breath. He didn't want to hear about her great love for some damn wonderful man she knew. He didn't want to hear about love at all. He only wanted to tumble her in bed. Feel her move beneath him, satisfy the growing need in him for her. Get her out of his system so he could get back to the important things in life, like buying the Triple T Ranch.

"That's none of your business," she said, pushing against his shoulder. She felt vulnerable and exposed. He still stood between her spread thighs, his hands moving to rest on her cotton skirt, her legs hot and tingling as he pinned her to the counter. She could feel the warmth from his body envelop hers, heat hers. And his raw masculinity was too distracting, too disturbing. Too enticing. If she planned to keep even a bit of her sanity, he had to leave. Now.

"Trace, move away."

"No." He lowered his head again, his lips toying with hers. God, he wanted this woman like he'd never wanted another.

"Trace, please." Her lips met his, responded. His mouth was firm, warm. Her tongue traced the shape of his lips, tasted him again and again. She slipped into his mouth even as she tried to clutch her sanity. Crazy beyond belief, she was burning up for more.

His hands moved beneath her top. He felt her jerk of surprise as he gently rubbed her soft, satiny skin. Slowly his hands pressed against her, his fingers and palm tingling with sensation. The softness of her skin was compelling. He never wanted to let go. Skimming across the ridges of her ribs, he moved to her breasts, feeling their slight weight, learning their shape. Feeling the thrust of her nipples against his palms, he sighed softly and kissed her again, openmouthed, hot. She was so feminine, so sweet. His blood heated to boiling. His desire strengthened until he could scarcely breathe.

"Dad?" Becky's voice called from outside.

Trace pulled back, his eyes flicked open and he stared into Kalli's dark gaze. "Becky, I thought I told you to go see Josh," he called back, his glittering gaze never leaving Kalli's.

"He's watching some dumb TV show." Her voice drew steadily closer.

Trace brought his hands down from Kalli's breasts and lifted her from the counter. Running fingers through his hair, he leaned into the counter, gripping the tile edge with hard fingers, keeping his back to the door as his daughter entered the kitchen, the screen slamming behind her.

"And I didn't want to see it." Becky looked suspiciously at Kalli, and then at her father.

"Your hair is all messed up," she said, glaring at Kalli.

"It's hot in here and the braid was confining," Kalli snapped, trying to draw some semblance of order to her tangled hair. In the throes of passion with Trace she'd been scarcely aware of his loosening the braid and fisting his hand in her hair.

"Are we going home now?" Becky asked her dad.

"Yeah, in a minute." He gripped the counter hard, and willed the blatant evidence of his desire for Kalli to fade so he could face his impressionable twelve-year-old daughter. Damn, why couldn't she have watched the blasted TV show with the men in the bunkhouse?

"Why are you standing there?" Becky asked.

Kalli glanced at Trace, instantly understanding.

"He's mad at me and probably holding onto the counter to keep from wrapping his hands around my neck," Kalli said easily, moving away from Trace, hoping to distract his daughter. "I have some cake I made for dessert. Would you like some before you go?"

"Why is he mad at you?" Becky asked, her suspicion growing as she looked back and forth.

"Because I won't sell him my ranch. It's chocolate cake."

"Yeah, I'd like some." Becky moved to the table.

"Is yeah a Wyoming way of saying yes, or just the way you and your father say it?" Kalli asked, desperate to keep some level of conversation going. She was so nervous around Trace, and embarrassed at almost being caught by his daughter. She wished they'd both leave, but she'd see the evening through. Time enough to get herself under control when they left.

"I don't know," Becky asked as she took the offered plate. "Daddy says it all the time."

"Yeah, I know," Kalli teased, sitting down, glad of the chair. Her legs trembled. She could still feel the imprint of Trace's hands on her thighs, her hips, her head, her breast. Heat suffused. It was all she could do to be polite.

"Do you want some cake, Trace?" Kalli asked politely.

"No." He turned and walked to the door, snatching up his hat. He paused and looked at Kalli, his eyes narrowed and intense.

"This isn't the end, Kalli. I'll get what I want."

As he left the kitchen, she shivered slightly. She knew he wasn't only talking about the ranch.

"When are you going back to Boston?" Becky asked as she finished the chocolate cake. Kalli poured her a glass of milk and the girl drank it, looking at Kalli with wise old eyes.

"I'm not."

"Dad says you are. We don't want you around here!"

"Why's that?" Kalli was a little surprised at the vehemence in Becky's tone. Why did the girl care one way or the other?

"He kissed you again, didn't he?" she asked. "Your mouth is all swollen and red."

Jealous? Kalli wondered, meeting the child's eyes. Becky was smart. Kalli nodded. She wasn't about to volunteer anything, but she wouldn't lie to this child.

"My mother was very beautiful, did you know?" Becky asked, pushing away her plate, then moving her glass before her. She chanced a glance at Kalli to see how she reacted to the news.

"I'm sure she was. Your father doesn't strike me as the type to go for homely women," she said dryly.

"I've seen a picture of them together. Daddy keeps it in his room. She was tall and blond and beautiful."

"I'm not out to replace your mother," Kalli said gently. Disturbed by the picture Becky painted, she frowned. If Trace really didn't care for his ex-wife, why keep her picture in his room? Especially after all these years. She'd been gone over a decade. Alyssa. What a pretty name, obviously in keeping with the pretty woman. Kalli refused to name the emotion that surfaced.

"I'm probably going to be as tall as her," Becky said proudly, unwilling to let the topic drop. "I'm already as tall as you and I'm only twelve."

"Then you'll be lucky. The only thing I'd change about myself is my height. It's awful being so short sometimes," Kalli murmured.

"Thank you for dinner, and the cake." Becky stood and started for the door. Pausing where her father had stood, she turned back. "And goodbye. I probably won't see you again."

"Goodbye, Becky. It was nice meeting you," Kalli said politely, wondering if she would see this child again. Not if she severed all relations with Trace. And she planned to do that the next time she saw him.

Which proved to be the very next morning at six o'clock when he banged on her bedroom door.

"Go away," Kalli called from beneath her pillow. She'd had a horrible night. Dream after dream had chased through her mind, waking her, making sleep virtually impossible. Every one of them concerned Trace. In some he chased her on a horse, six-guns drawn, running her out of the county. In others he kissed her, rubbing his work-rough hands over her hot body, watching her as she gave in to the urging he constantly whispered in her ear. Those had been the worst.

"Rise and shine, Boss Lady. You've got a ranch to run."

"Dammit." She got up and stormed to the door, flinging it wide. "Right you are, cowboy! This is my ranch and I'll run it and I'll start by beginning the day at a reasonable hour!"

He grinned at her. She looked good enough to eat, rosy from sleep, her dark eyes snapping and sparkling and her hair tousled every which way around her head. Glancing over her shoulders, he almost groaned when he saw the tumbled sheets on her bed, the impression of her head clearly visible on one of the pillows.

"A reasonable hour? Sweetheart, it's six."

"That's right, and I like to see six o'clock in the morning from bed."

"Fine." He dropped his hat and reached out to scoop her up. In only two seconds he dumped her on her bed and followed her down, his hard chest pinning her to the mattress as his hands cupped her face, fingertips threading in her tangled hair. His mouth came down hard on hers.

Kalli was astonished. Then complacent, then hot and bothered and turned on and wanting more of this wild cowboy who wouldn't take no for an answer to anything. Her bare legs felt the roughness of his denims and the scrape of his boot. His belt buckle pressed into her soft skin. He was heavy and hard. But all conscious thought fled as his mouth made sweet love to hers. As he brought her to a state of awareness and desire beyond anything she'd felt before. Instead of pushing him away, instead of becoming irate he'd thrust his way into her room, she ran her hands up his arms, across the broad shoulders, sculpting the shape of his muscles, squirming a bit beneath him to get more comfortable, reveling in the taste and scent of him.

She was as soft as down. As sweet as honeysuckle. He would devour her with his mouth if he could. She was so sweet, so hot and so compliant. Why the change? He expected fireworks from her, and he was getting them, but not *this* way.

His hand trailed down her throat, across her shoulder. Feeling the soft cotton of her T-shirt, for a moment he envied it. The shirt covered her torso completely, draped over every curve and mound and valley. Just as he wanted to drape himself over her. Learn every inch of her, cover every inch of her, taste every inch of her. His fingers traced down farther, feeling the soft swell of the side of her breast, flattened because of his weight. Rolling over slightly, he freed her. Freed her for his touch. His hand kneaded her softness through the cotton, wanting to feel that impudent nipple against his palm again, wanting to feel her bare skin against his.

His knee slipped between hers and he pushed his thigh into the notch between her legs. Rubbing his fingers across her waist, he pulled up the T-shirt, his knuckles brushing against her hip. The softness tantalized his fingertips, sent a longing deep in his gut to absorb every part of that soft skin against his own tougher hide.

"Hell." He pulled back and stared into her glazed eyes as his fingers moved against her hip. "You're not even wearing panties."

She shook her head, too bemused to speak. Her eyes soft with passion, her body hot and craving.

Slowly his hand moved across her abdomen, down to feather against the soft curls, lower, lower still.

She held her breath, staring at him in unconscious hunger.

"Don't, Trace. You need to leave." But her hands gave lie to her words. They still gripped him. One moved across his shoulders, down to the V of his shirt, one finger rubbing sensuously against the copper skin of his chest.

"You don't want me to leave," he said softly, his fingers finding her, softly stroking her. Her hips rose, fell.

"You don't even like me," she whispered, finding and releasing one button. Swamped by sweet hot sensations that built and built.

"I like you," he murmured, brushing a kiss against her damp swollen lips. His finger stroked again, gently parted her.

She caught her breath, her eyes wide with wonder and delight. Then she frowned, tried to close her legs, but his hard thigh prevented it.

"Don't," she said again.

"Yeah." His finger moved again, and again, gently, slowly, sweetly.

Her gaze never left his, except when he'd lower his head to kiss her gently. It was heady. The raw sex urge had faded, and an exquisitely tortuous one remained, slow, achingly sweet and just as demanding.

His finger slipped in.

She caught another breath, shook her head slightly.

"Trace. I'm not ready for something like this."

"Just this, sweetheart. Just this." His finger moved again. A second joined the first.

"It's not right," she breathed, almost unable to talk, to reason. The feelings that coursed through her were delectable. She shivered as the sensations shimmered throughout. She caught the rhythm of his hand, feeling every inch of the fingers that played her as if she was a delicate instrument.

"Nothing is wrong with a man and woman wanting each other if they are attracted and they both agree to it."

"You're . . . getting . . . nothing out of this." Her hand had opened his shirt. Her greedy palm rubbed the defined muscles of his chest, her fingers rubbed his nipple.

He was a perfect man. His body perfect beneath her hand. His knowledge of her perfect, just as the feel of his fingers against her caused the most exquisite sensations.

"Oh, yes, I am, sweetheart. Relax and enjoy it. I'm getting a lot out of this."

"But you could get more."

"Not yet, you said. Besides, there are a bunch of men outside waiting for us. We don't have time."

"Oh, no." She closed her eyes, all thought of her ranch, her position as boss, the threat of takeover by Trace forgotten as his fingers moved her higher.

He kissed her, his hand moving harder now, faster. "Come on, Kalli, let go. It'll be so perfect."

So perfect, she repeated as her body gave in to his urging and moved as he directed, fought him, surrendered to him, accepted the glorious gift of his hand and mouth. The waves of ecstasy coursed through her, flooding her senses, filling her with heat and fire and delight. When he felt her first contractions, he lay across her, feeling the undulation of her body, his mouth capturing her cries, his body aching to know the fulfillment she would one day bring him. For now this would have to be enough. But one day she would want all of him and he would not deny her.

Kalli was floating. Vaguely she felt his hand withdraw and his thigh press against her, hard. The fingers moved her shirt up, exposing her damp skin to the morning coolness. In only a second his hot mouth captured her nipple and sucked into the hot cavern. She rolled slightly to offer it more fully, her arms so weak she could scarcely move them. Trace kissed her other breast, his lips moving across the damp skin of her stomach to the dampness between her legs, back to her mouth.

She sighed and kissed him. Feeling the hard ridge of his desire, she opened her eyes slightly and gazed into his heated ones.

"Are you okay?" he asked.

She nodded solemnly. She'd never felt so good in her life, but felt guilty at enjoying herself and not giving him any release. "But you—"

"I'm fine." He pressed his hip against hers, knowing she felt his hardness, then smiled. "One day you're going to say yes to everything."

"Or *yeah*," she said sassily, touched at his gentleness. This was not the angry man of last night. Not the ruthless neighbor who wanted nothing but her land. This man was deeper than that. Complex. She wished she knew him better.

God, if she knew him any better, he'd be naked on top of her, inside her, a part of her.

"That bunch of men you mentioned . . ." she started.

"Yeah. They'll be looking for us soon. Get dressed. I'll fix us something to eat. We've got a lot to do today."

"In case it escaped you, I fired you yesterday," she reminded him, loath to have him leave. She felt sheltered and well-loved.

"Yeah, I remember you saying something like that, but knew you didn't mean it. You can't run this place and I don't want it ruined before I take over."

"You're not taking over." The well-loved feeling fled.

"Sooner or later you're going to give up and then I'll get it. If you want to stay a while, I don't have a problem with it. But let me keep the place going, keep it up."

"What if I stay forever?"

"You won't."

"You don't know that!" He made her so mad. She was not Alyssa!

"No, I don't." He took her hands, one at a time, and laced his hands through them, raising them over her head as he settled himself down along the length of her. "But I don't think you'll last. What's the harm? If you do stay, you'll have a top-notch ranch. If you go, I'll get a place in good repair and profitable, not something that's been left to decay.''

What could it hurt? She needed the help, she knew it. And if he volunteered, why not take him up on it. He'd find out sooner or later that she was in for the long haul. Let him help her.

"But no sex," she said, capitulating.

He leaned down and kissed her, long and leisurely, his tongue's forays into her mouth causing her to tighten all over.

The situation was positively decadent. She was lying practically naked beneath him, and he was fully clothed. She moved experimentally. She could feel every inch of him, and it was driving her crazy. She wanted him. She wanted him almost as badly as he seemed to want her. She felt naughty and delighted and oh, so erotic.

"Oh, yeah, sweetheart, we'll have sex. As often as you allow it. I told you, it has nothing to do with ownership of the ranch.''

Five

Trace stared out the kitchen window, sipping the hot coffee that had just been brewed. Josh and Tim were loading barbed wire into the back of his truck. The tools had been tossed in a few minutes earlier. Charlie came out of the bunkhouse and hurried over to the men.

Shifting slightly, Trace tried to ease his tight jeans. They normally fit fine, but just being around Kalli caused them to shrink several sizes.

Kalli. He could still feel her moving against him. Feel the heat from her body, the ecstatic little sounds she made while she was writhing beneath him. Hell, if the men hadn't been getting ready for the day's work, if they hadn't been waiting for him in the yard, he'd have shucked his jeans and made long, slow love to her all morning.

He shook his head, took another sip of the scalding coffee as he clenched his free hand into a fist. Damn, she wasn't some long-legged blond beauty like the women he normally favored. She wasn't bigger than a minute, and was as dark as he was. She didn't make up to him as if he was some blasted hero like the girls who had followed the rodeos. What was she thinking about in that pretty head of hers?

Hell, he had no business thinking about her at all. Not in bed. He had to get rid of her. He wanted this ranch. He didn't want some entanglement with a feisty little lady with stars in her eyes and boundless optimism. Life in Wyoming was rough. Life on a ranch rougher. She wouldn't last two weeks.

Why not enjoy her however long she does last? The insidious thought crept into his mind. He couldn't shake it. He had been a long time without a woman. It wasn't easy with a young child. Especially a girl. And not many women around wanted anything to do with a casual, part-time affair. If he knew anything, it was that women always wanted to tie the man up in knots, get their kicks, then move on to the next sucker. Just like Alyssa had.

He threw out the rest of his coffee and headed for the yard. One night. That's all he wanted. One night to get her out of his system before she left. Then he'd go back to wanting leggy blondes who knew the score.

Kalli dawdled as long as she dared in getting dressed. She couldn't believe her response to Trace's invasion of her bedroom. She couldn't believe she had permitted the intimacy he'd instituted, actually reveled in it. She was still flushed, her heart rate still rapid just thinking about it. About him.

The cool shower had not damped down the heat deep within her. Dressing only reminded her of the sensuous feel of his clothes against her body. Brushing her hair reminded her of his fingers tangled in the thickness, of the feel of his hands holding her head, caressing her, drawing the long strands through his roughened fingertips as if savoring the very feel of each shaft.

Finally she could stall no longer. He said everyone was waiting, what did they think she was doing? With a final look in the mirror, she groaned. Her eyes were bright, the color high in her cheeks, her lips slightly swollen. She looked well loved!

Loved, ha. There was no love between them. Trace wanted one thing, her ranch. She had better never lose sight of that. Kisses and caresses and lovemaking were tools to achieve his goal, not the reflection of some deep abiding affection for her. Just because his very presence made her feel more alive than ever before, just because being with him was more exciting than anything she'd ever experienced was no reason to lose control. To forfeit everything just to gain his approval.

She tried to work up her anger, tried to feel used. She knew he only wanted her ranch. But she felt glorious. And deep inside she wished he'd kiss her again, hot and wet and, oh, so devastating, just like he'd kissed her this morning.

"Dumb move, Kalli," she muttered as she left her room. Angry now, but at herself for her own gullibility, she stormed to the kitchen.

There was no sign of Trace. The coffee had been made, and its lingering aroma filled the room. There was a dirty cup on the counter. Crossing to the window, she peered out. Trace was talking with Tim. The other men were busy loading his truck. A second pickup truck was parked beside Trace's, its bed already piled high.

Taking a deep breath, Kalli moved to join them.

"Good morning, ma'am," Josh called. The others greeted her cheerfully.

"Good morning." She smiled at each man. They had no problem with her owning the ranch. They'd been nothing but polite and enthusiastic when dealing with her. But she avoided Trace's eyes. She just couldn't face him after what they'd done just a few minutes before.

Her skin tingled at his proximity. She longed to take a quick peek at his face, just to see if he was feeling any of the myriad emotions that chased through her. But she was afraid she'd only see the impassive expression that hid all feelings. He was so good at that.

"What are we doing today?" she asked, taking in the rolls of barbed wire in the back of Trace's big truck.

"Fixing some of the fencing," Trace replied. He nodded to Josh and Tim. "They'll take that truck and work along the wash near the river. Charlie, José and I will take mine and work near the Flying Cloud boundary."

She looked at his chin. "Wouldn't want any Triple T stock to wander on that land, now, would we? Might give the owner ideas. I'll go with Josh and Tim, then." She turned to glance at the dusty truck.

"Nope. You'll stay here today."

She swung back to meet his eyes at that, startled at the look he gave her.

"I'm not—"

"Shut up, Kalli. You'll do as you're told. You stay here and bring the records up to date."

"Forget it, I'm going. Might I remind you, Trace, that this is still *my* ranch and—"

"Excuse me, boys, I'll be right back." So saying, he gripped her upper arm, turned her smartly around and hurried her to the kitchen, not saying a word until the screen door banged behind them.

"Trace, you can't tell me—"

"Kalli, for once since I've known you, be sensible. You can't work on fencing, you wouldn't have a clue what to do. It's too dangerous. That's why you have hired hands. You pay them for doing that kind of work. Anyway, you need to get the records caught up. Once they are, the process won't take much upkeep."

"I'm the owner here, I'll say what I can and can't do. You're so bossy! You don't own this place."

"Yet."

"Never! If I want to help with the fencing, I'll do it!" He made her so angry sometimes she wanted to spit. "Why's the fencing dangerous?"

"First of all, you're not big enough. It's demanding, physical work. If the wire snaps when being pulled taut, it can whip around like a knife blade, cutting anything in its way."

She glared at him and opened her mouth to set him straight when he ruthlessly continued without giving her a second to speak.

"Second, it's almost payday. Don't you think you should get your records up to date so you'll know if you have enough money in the bank to pay the men?"

She blinked, stared at him, thinking furiously. Put like that, it made some sort of sense. She didn't want it to—she wanted to say she'd work the fencing if she damned well pleased. But she wasn't a fool. And truth to tell, she was still stiff and sore from all the recent riding she'd done. Heat flashed through her as she thought of the aching muscles she'd ignored earlier when they'd been on her bed.

"I'm sure I have enough money," she grumbled, tugging on her arm. She wanted to put some distance between them lest she fling herself against him and beg for another kiss. Or sock him once for being so damned bossy. "How did they get paid before?"

"From the estate, Richard paid them from the account. Now that you're officially signed on, you have to pay them."

"How did you know..." She trailed off. Small town news. Was nothing secret around here?

"We'll be gone most of the day. Will you be okay here alone?" he asked, his fingers easing their grip, moving slowly along her arm, feeling her warmth beneath the cotton of her shirt.

"Of course." She drew herself up to her full five feet two inches and tilted her chin.

He nodded, his eyes dark and fathomless. Slowly he leaned over and brushed his mouth against hers.

Don't kiss him back, Kalli told herself, even as her own lips softened and parted slightly.

He pulled away and released her, turning to leave.

"Trace?" she called.

"Yeah?"

"Don't let any barbed wire snap."

He nodded and left.

Kalli walked to the window and watched as the men finished loading what they needed, then climbed into the two trucks and drove away. Once the sound of the engines faded, it was still, quiet. Feeling lonely for the first time in ages, Kalli turned to fix her breakfast, torn between being angry at Trace for telling her what to do, and oddly pleased he was protective of her.

Not that it changed anything. She would learn all she could about ranching, to free herself of her dependence on him. Her uncle had left the ranch to her. She would make it work on her own! And her attraction to the rugged rancher who wanted her land would take second place. If he could keep the two issues separate, so could she.

By midafternoon she was almost blind from working at the computer. She saved all she'd done and leaned back in the chair, massaging her aching shoulders and neck muscles. God, she was tired. Staring out the window to ease the strain in her eyes, she smiled. The sight was breathtaking. The granite of the Grand Tetons rose mightily in the distance, stark and rugged against the clear blue sky. The hills were green with spring grass, the aspen near the house shivered in some unseen breeze.

Slowly she stretched. She felt better, not so stiff. Maybe she'd go for a short ride. Maybe even ride out and see how the fencing was coming. Of course, there was the problem of saddling the horse. She'd have to figure something out.

She clicked off the computer and went to put on her boots. In only moments she was ready. As Kalli left the house using the back door, Becky Longford rode into the yard, her small Appaloosa filly just the right size for her.

"Hello," Kalli said as the youngster drew up near her. She should see about getting a smaller mount like Becky's.

"Hi. I came to see my dad," Becky said, looking around toward the barn.

"He's out fixing fences," Kalli said.

"Oh. Do you know where?"

"On the property line between our two ranches, I think. Didn't you see him as you rode over?"

"I came around the road for the most part. It's not too far that way. Which way did they go?" Becky asked.

"If you want to wait a minute, I was just going to go for a ride myself. I could ride with you for company if you like." And see Trace.

Becky hesitated a moment, then shrugged. "Sure. Why not?" She turned her horse toward the barn, walking alongside Kalli. "Need any help saddling your horse?" The offer surprised Kalli.

"I could use some." When Kalli reached the barn she waited by the door while Becky dismounted and tied her horse to the corral rail. The girl was as tall as Kalli. Did she saddle her own horse?

"Which horse do you want?" Becky asked, looking through the rails into the corral. There were several horses dozing in the afternoon sun.

"I don't know. Does it matter?" Kalli asked.

Becky looked at her for a moment. "I guess not. Which one did you ride before?"

"A brown one."

Becky rolled her eyes and looked at the horses milling around. "Most of them are brown. Did you ride Stony or Billy or Roman?"

"I don't know. Whatever one your father saddled for me." Kalli came to study the horses, trying to remember which one she'd ridden before. They all looked alike to her, big.

"Then we'll take Stony," Becky announced, climbing the fence. In only a few minutes, she had the horse tied to the top rail and was bringing out a saddle, blanket and bridle.

"I can help," Kalli said, reaching for the blanket and the bridle. She already knew the saddle was too heavy. How did Becky manage?

"Getting on is a problem. How do you mount?" she asked as Becky dumped the saddle beside the horse.

"I find a fence or stump or something, if I'm away from home. Can you saddle him?"

"I know how, but the saddle's too heavy."

"Do what you can and I'll help you lift the saddle," Becky said, stepping back. Her expression was challenging.

Think I can't do this? Kalli thought as she stepped up to the big horse. Before long she had the bridle on, took the blanket from Becky and flung it in place.

"How do you manage to saddle your horse?" Kalli asked as she struggled with the heavy Western saddle.

"Dad built me a platform. I cross tie the horse beside it to groom him and tack him up. Here, you'll never get it on that way." Becky helped her swing the heavy saddle onto the horse's back. Once it was in place, the horse shied away.

Reaching beneath him, Kalli drew up the cinch, began tightening it. The horse blew from his nostrils, side-stepped again, dancing nervously in the dusty corral.

Persevering, Kalli cinched it tight, flipped down the stirrups.

"Climb on the rails and step into the saddle," Becky suggested, squirming through the rails and going to her horse, watching Kalli as she walked.

Kalli tried to bring Stony near the rail, but he was skittish, sidestepping, dancing, moving. Finally he was close enough. She climbed the wooden fence, stepped into the stirrup and swung her leg over quickly before he could move away.

Scarcely had her bottom touched the saddle before the horse exploded. He threw up his hind legs, humped his back and jerked around. Head lowered, he bucked again and again. Kalli felt herself leave the saddle, slam down hard on her bottom.

The second time she attempted to sit the horse, he moved from beneath her. One minute she was on him, the next she was floating through the air. Her foot caught in the stirrup and held. She came down on her shoulder, feeling the twisting in her ankle before the horse jumped to the side, dislodging her boot before she could be dragged across the soft, dry dirt. Her hip hit hard. Stunned by the unexpectedness of it all, Kalli lay still, trying to catch her breath, trying to see if she'd broken anything.

She'd heard Becky's laughter when she first mounted the horse. Now there was only silence.

"Kalli?" Becky came flying through the fence and over to her. "Kalli? Are you dead?" Her voice was scared.

Kalli opened her eyes and looked at the girl. "No. I'm not dead." But by tomorrow she'd probably wish she was. She felt as if she was one gigantic bruise already. Gingerly she moved, tried to sit up. "I don't even think I broke anything. What happened?" She leaned toward her right hip, easing the pain in her left one. Her left shoulder was throbbing, her whole body tightened and began to ache. Looking around, she saw the other horses mildly watching her. Her hat was several feet away. She rolled to her knees and tried to stand.

"Ow!" Sinking back into the dirt, she clutched her left ankle. She had definitely twisted it. Glancing around, she saw Stony standing several yards away, still nervous, his eyes on her, blowing hard.

"Stony bucked and you came flying off," Becky said, sitting back and watching Kalli worriedly. "Are you all right?"

"Shouldn't you get the horse? I don't want him bucking his way back over here," Kalli said, her wary eyes never leaving Stony.

Becky walked up to the skittish horse and grabbed his reins. In only moments she had him unsaddled and turned him free. She put the equipment away, casting worried glances at Kalli all the while.

"Can you get to the house? Should I ride for my dad?" she asked when she came back.

Kalli almost groaned. The last thing she needed was for Trace to find her here. He thought so poorly of her ranching abilities, this would only confirm his bad opinion. "No, don't tell your father. If you could help me up, I can hop to the house." She got on her knees again, careful of her injured foot. She stood on her good leg, using Becky as a support. Slowly they made their way to the gate, through it and to the house. Every hop jarred through her. Her entire left side felt on fire.

"Horses buck sometimes, you know," Becky said as she helped Kalli. "You have to watch for that and be ready. I never get bucked off," she said proudly. "Neither does my dad."

"Well, bully for both of you. I'm still new at this."

"You don't belong here. I heard my dad saying that. You should go home. This just shows you can't be a rancher. Ranchers never get bucked off."

Kalli wasn't going to argue with her. At this moment, she wasn't too sure Becky wasn't right.

They made it as far as the kitchen table, where Kalli pulled out a chair and sank down, her shoulder throbbing, her ankle white-hot agony, her hip aching. God, she was a mess. Would a warm bath help? Then ice for the bruises? She wondered if she could even make it as far as her bathroom. How would she ever manage getting into and out of a bath?

The throaty roar of a pickup truck sounded in the distance, grew louder until it was right outside. Kalli felt her insides tighten. Maybe it would be Charlie. Maybe he could help her into her room.

"It's Dad," Becky said with a smile. Hurrying from the house, she flew out to meet her father.

"Dad, you better come see to that city lady. She fell and hurt herself. Probably needs to go into town and see a doctor," Becky said as soon as he drew to a halt.

"What happened?" Trace forgot his curiosity at Becky's being here at her words. For a moment he felt sick. What had happened to Kalli? Was she all right? Did she really need a doctor?

"Come see." Becky turned and ran inside, Trace only inches behind her.

Kalli looked defiant as she sat in the chair, her left leg crossed over her right knee. Her clothes were dusty, there was a smudge on one cheek and her eyes were bright with unshed tears.

"What did you do to yourself?" he asked as he drew near, leaned over her.

Blinking her eyes to keep the tears at bay, she tried a smile. "Just took a little tumble off a horse. Nothing a big rodeo star would even notice," she said.

"Ah, hell, honey. Did you get hurt?"

She nodded, prepared for his sarcasm, not prepared for his concern. "I think I twisted my ankle."

His hands reached out and felt along the boot, firmly, yet gently. She winced at his touch, catching her breath at the pain that coursed up her leg.

"It's already swollen. How did it happen?"

He continued to examine her foot, ankle, leg as she told him about her aborted attempt to ride. When he finished, he looked into her shimmering eyes.

Trace's heart slammed against his chest. He hurt that she hurt. He wanted to snatch her up and ease the pain away. Shelter her so she never got hurt again. She wasn't any bigger than Becky. She needed to be cared for, cherished. Why was she being so foolish, insisting on continuing in this quest to own and operate a cattle ranch? Dammit, she was as unsuited for this as he was for a boardroom in Boston.

"I told her ranchers didn't fall off horses," Becky said, sidling up to her dad and staring at Kalli.

"I didn't fall, Stony bucked me off," Kalli clarified.

"Stony?" Trace asked in disbelief. "He's as gentle as they come."

"Well, if he's so gentle, I'd like to see some wild stock."

Gently Trace tugged on her boot. A white-hot lance of pain shot through her leg.

"Ow! Dammit, Trace, what are you trying to do, rip my foot off?" Tears spilled over and coursed down her dirty cheek. The pain was worse now. What was he, some sort of sadist?

"Just seeing how bad it is. We'll have to cut off your boot. There's no way we can pull it off if that little tug hurt so bad."

"Not my new boots," she protested.

"I'm open for other suggestions," he said as he rose and fetched a knife from the cutlery drawer.

She watched him approach, then looked sadly at her fancy Western boots. She'd been so excited to buy them.

So excited she needed boots where she was going. She'd only had them a couple of weeks.

"I'll buy you another pair," he said sardonically as he knelt beside her. Tossing his hat on the table, he slipped the blade down between her leg and the boot top, cutting the soft leather as if it was butter.

She gritted her teeth. She knew he was trying to be careful, but it still hurt. Finally the boot was off. Instantly she felt better.

He rose and picked her up. As he turned to head for her room, he told Becky to fix up an ice pack.

Shouldering open the door to her room, he noticed she'd made the bed. For a second his eyes met hers and they both remembered that morning.

Slowly he lowered her to the mattress, taking care to keep her foot from jarring.

She lay back, moaned slightly and turned toward her right.

"What else?" he asked.

"I landed on my shoulder, I guess it's bruised, too." He unbuttoned her shirt and drew it down her arms. The pale skin of her shoulder showed an ugly purple patch larger than his hand.

Kalli gripped the front of her shirt across her breasts. She looked at her shoulder and frowned. "I'm sure it's just bruised."

He took her arm, releasing her grip on the material, and rotated it slowly, gently. "How's that?"

"Just great, Doctor." It pulled a little, but she was sure nothing was broken.

"I may not be a doctor, but I do know a little about injuries people get from being thrown. I probably have more experience at it than most of your Bostonian doctors put together."

She grinned. "You probably do. First hand, too, I'd bet."

"You'd win."

"Here's the ice." Becky stood in the doorway, watching warily.

Trace stood up and turned to get it. He met her eyes, his own cautious.

"Are you taking her into town?" she asked her dad.

"No."

"But she probably needs to see a doctor. And then she can go home."

"Home?"

"She's not a rancher, Dad. You said so, and today proves it. She should just go back to Boston and let you have the ranch."

Trace smiled and ruffled her hair. "She should, pumpkin, but my bet is she won't."

"And you'd win," Kalli called, annoyed that even his daughter wanted her gone.

Becky looked around her father at Kalli, anger and frustration in her expression. "If my dad didn't help you out, you'd be gone in a flash. You don't know nothing about ranching."

"That's enough Becky," Trace said sharply. He set the ice pack on the edge of the bed and looked at Kalli. "Where do you keep your nightgowns?"

"I sleep in T-shirts," she said, remembering that morning. "In the second drawer, on the left." Suddenly the aches and pains fled. She could only watch as Trace opened her bureau drawer. She imagined his eyes on the frilly underwear lying beside the practical cotton T-shirts she'd taken from her brothers.

He withdrew a navy shirt with Boston Red Sox in big red letters.

"Whose was this?" It was obviously a man's shirt. Who did she know intimately enough to use his shirt to sleep in? His gut tightened, and his hand fisted around the shirt.

"That one's my brother Pete's," she said.

His eyes met hers. *And the one this morning?*

As clearly as if he'd said it, she knew what he was asking. Smiling a little, she whispered, "I also have some from my brother Mark."

He tossed her the shirt, relief spreading through him. "Can you manage by yourself, or do you need help?"

"I can manage."

"How about your jeans?"

Her jeans. How would she get them off without jarring her ankle?

"Becky, go look in the bathroom for some aspirin. Get her a glass of water, too," Trace ordered.

When she was gone, he reached out to help Kalli. He unfastened the snap, drew down the zipper. Ignoring the pale pink panties that scarcely covered her, he lifted her hips and eased the denim over them. Settling her back on the bed, he gently peeled the jeans from her, taking care with her injured ankle. Sweat broke out on his forehead with the effort he made to keep his eyes from seeking the dark shadow behind the pale pink lace. Her thighs were slender, shapely, soft. Her foot was small, delicate, like the rest of her, he noted as he eased the socks off. His fingers ached to brush across that satiny skin, to trail up to the apex of her thighs and again feel her deep, fiery heat.

Kalli clutched the navy T-shirt against her, trying to hide her breasts, feeling disoriented and shaky inside. She knew he was only helping her out, but the touch of his hands against her legs was almost more than she could stand.

His gaze met hers, held. The fire that had been banked began to build again. He leaned forward slowly and pulled her into a sitting position, his eyes never leaving hers. As if in slow motion, he reached behind her and released her bra. Pulling the T-shirt from her lifeless fingers, he opened her shirt, pulling it and the bra from her. She was so beautiful. Her breasts were firm and plump, crowned with dusty pink nipples that were already tight with promise. She was so slender and soft, like the brush of the sweetest wildflower in spring.

Trace wanted to touch her, feel the silken texture of her soft skin. Taste the unique flavors of her body. Lose himself in her and forget everything. But he heard the running water in the bathroom, knew his daughter would be back in only seconds. Regretfully, he handed Kalli the T-shirt and rose, taking three difficult steps away.

Kalli also heard the water, knew Becky would be back in an instant. She yanked on the T-shirt, wincing only slightly as her sore shoulder strained against the fabric. Once safely covered, she drew the side of the coverlet over her bare legs. It didn't cover her feet and she stared at her swollen ankle, already twice the size of her other one.

While Becky folded Kalli's clothes and laid them on a nearby chair, Trace found a scarf and bound up her ankle. "That'll have to do until later. We have a complete first-aid kit at home and I'll get an Ace bandage to immobilize your foot. If you're not feeling better in the morning, maybe we'll take a run into town and have it x-rayed."

"It's only sprained. It already feels better," Kalli said, settling back against her pillows. She ached from head to foot, and probably would for a couple of days. But she wasn't seriously injured. And was still in charge of her ranch. She hoped Trace understood that.

"Thank you for all your help," she told them.

Trace nodded, reluctant to leave. She looked so small, so helpless in the big bed. How would she manage?

"Trace, before you leave, tell Charlie and Josh, okay? Then they can come check on me," Kalli said.

Like hell they would. There was no way he was going to let those rough cowboys in to see her in her bed. See her in those soft T-shirts that molded her figure like a second skin. Let them see her silky legs, indecent panties.

"I'll be back to fix your supper, make sure you are okay for the night."

"No need. One of the men can see to it."

"I'll be back!"

Six

When Kalli awoke, it was dark. She lay still in the quiet night, loath to move. She ached from head to toe. Her ankle throbbed lightly, enough to let her know it was sore, but not enough to wake her. Her shoulder was tender. She rolled over, stifling a moan. She sat up on the edge of the bed. Slowly she rose, hopped to the bathroom, each step jarring her already hurting body.

On her way back, the hall light flicked on, then the door to her room, which had been left slightly ajar, was pushed open. Trace stood silhouetted in the frame.

"What are you doing?" he asked, taking in her disheveled appearance, her tousled hair, the T-shirt that fell to her thighs, the bent leg she was trying to keep from touching the floor.

"I needed the bathroom. What are you doing here?" she asked belligerently, holding onto the door jamb to the bath. The best offense, she told herself as she felt a wave of pure pleasure crash over her at the sight of him.

"Taking care of you." He walked across the room and swept her up into his arms. Turning, he began walking to the bed.

"I don't want to go back to bed. I've been asleep for hours and I'm hungry," she said, encircling his neck with one arm, trying to maintain some sane distance between them. Which was about as easy as staying on a bucking horse. She was, out of necessity, pressed tight against his chest. The strong arms that held her locked in place were warm beneath her bare legs, through the thin cotton of her shirt. His face was only inches from her hers. She could see the small lines radiating from his dark eyes, and could smell his tangy scent.

He hesitated then turned toward the open door. "I'll fix you something to eat."

"I thought I told you to tell Charlie or Josh about me. Charlie could have brought me something for dinner."

"I have no intention of letting a bunch of randy cowboys raid your room with you dressed like this," he muttered as they reached the kitchen. She didn't weigh anything. She could stand to gain a few more pounds.

"I'm the owner here," she said impotently. Randy cowboys? The only one randy around here was her, and only when he was so close. Shyly she let her fingers touch his neck. That's all. Just a touch. But she didn't expect the tingling to spread throughout her body from where her fingertips touched him.

"You're the owner, but I give the orders," Trace replied as he gently placed her in a chair. "What do you want to eat?"

"What does it matter, you'll decide and feed me whatever you want."

"Don't sulk, it's unbecoming," he chided gently. In only minutes he was cutting vegetables and cheese for an omelet.

SILHOUETTE®

AN IMPORTANT MESSAGE
FROM THE EDITORS OF
SILHOUETTE®

Dear Reader,

Because you've chosen to read one of our fine romance novels, we'd like to say "thank you"! And, as a **special** way to thank you, we've selected <u>four more</u> of the <u>books</u> you love so well, **and** a Porcelain Trinket Box to send you absolutely *FREE!*

Please enjoy them with our compliments...

Luna Macro

Senior Editor,
Silhouette Desire

P.S. And because we value our customers, we've attached something extra inside ...

PEEL OFF SEAL AND
PLACE INSIDE

THE EDITOR'S "THANK YOU" FREE GIFTS INCLUDE:

▶ Four BRAND-NEW romance novels
▶ A Porcelain Trinket Box

DETACH AND MAIL CARD TODAY!

YES! I have placed my Editor's "thank you" seal in the space provided above. Please send me 4 free books and a Porcelain Trinket Box. I understand I am under no obligation to purchase any books, as explained on the back and on the opposite page.

326 CIS AW7A (C-SIL-D-01/96)

_____

NAME

_____

ADDRESS   APT.

_____

CITY   PROVINCE   POSTAL CODE

Thank you!

THE SILHOUETTE READER SERVICE™: HERE'S HOW IT WORKS

Accepting free books places you under no obligation to buy anything. You may keep the books and gift and return the shipping statement marked "cancel". If you do not cancel, about a month later we will send you 6 additional novels, and bill you just $2.74 each plus 25¢ delivery and GST*. That's the complete price, and—compared to cover prices of $3.75 each—quite a bargain! You may cancel at any time, but if you choose to continue, every month we'll send you 6 more books, which you may either purchase at the discount price...or return at our expense and cancel your subscription.

*Terms and prices subject to change without notice. Canadian residents add applicable provincial taxes and GST.

SILHOUETTE READER SERVICE
PO BOX 609
FORT ERIE, ONT
L2A 9Z9

019561919199-L2A5X3-BR01

MAIL ▷ POSTE
Canada Post Corporation / Société canadienne des postes
Postage paid   Port payé
if mailed in Canada   si posté au Canada
Business   Réponse
Reply   d'affaires
019561919199   01

"I'm not sulking. You frustrate me to death, Trace," she grumbled, watching him work. It seemed odd to have such a blatantly masculine male in her kitchen, cooking for her. For all his smoothness in the task, he looked out of place. In fact, just being inside made him seem out of place. He belonged to the rugged Wyoming land. He reminded her of the mountains in the distance, hard, demanding, tough and enduring.

Enduring. She studied him, noting the dark hair that gleamed in the overhead light. The teak skin, taut over high cheekbones, bronzed by endless days in the sun. She felt a quickening deep within her as if her body called to his. As if his called to hers and she replied. Mesmerized, she watched his hands slice tomatoes, then dice the Cheddar cheese. Those long, hard fingers had stroked her so gently. Had tended to her so tenderly. What a dichotomy the man was. Hard as granite, determined and stubborn, yet gentle as a baby when the occasion demanded.

"Frustrated, eh?" he repeated, a slow smile building. "I can take care of that, sweetheart, after you eat."

"Dammit! That's not what I mean and you know it. You never listen to me. I keep telling you I'm here for good and you act as if I'm on a visit and sooner or later will up and leave. I keep telling you this is my place, and I'll run it, and you ignore me as if I was a pesky fly. I'm tired of it."

"What do you expect?" He put the knife down and stared at her. "You got this ranch in a fluke of chance, like winning a high-stakes poker game. You don't know anything about ranching or cattle. You don't even have a business background. If lack of knowledge isn't enough, you don't belong out here. You're a *nurse*. From Boston. You're a city girl. The loneliness and solitude of Wyoming will get to you before long. You'd never last a winter here, snowbound for weeks on end, no nearby neighbors, no parties, stores, movies. Nothing but end-less cold and wind and snow."

She banged her fist on the table. "You don't know anything about me. I want to be here! I will make a go of it. I won't leave at the first sign of trouble. If I did, I would have been long gone by now, because trouble is all you've given me. I'm sorry you didn't get the ranch like you wanted. I'm sorry to be in your way, but Uncle Philip owned it all these years and you survived. You'll survive without the ranch now. I'm here to stay, so leave me alone!"

He straightened. Slowly he nodded. "Right. That's what I should have done all along. Leave you alone. More than anything, a woman can't stand to be left alone."

She boiled up at that. "Go to hell! You think you're irresistible, well, I can resist with the best of them."

"Like you did this morning?" he said sardonically, his eyes black as ink, threatening her with their harsh stare.

The fight went out of her instantly and her face broke. She blinked back tears at the insult, her gaze dropping to the hands fisted in her lap. "That was special," she said softly, painfully. The doubts rose again. Had he only been trying to seduce her because of the ranch? Had it meant nothing to him?

She spoke so softly he almost didn't hear her. But he did and felt as if she'd kicked him in the gut. The rage that warred in him at her attack eased. He wasn't really angry with her, he was angry at fate. She should never have inherited this ranch. If she hadn't, he would never have met her and his life would have been infinitely eas-ier. He knew better than to trust a woman. To care for a woman. Someone who would say one thing and mean another.

But he was attracted to this petite dark-haired woman like no other. And he didn't like it. He wanted her gone.

Wanted the disruption to his life ended. Wanted things back to normal. Lonely and dull, maybe, but with his heart and pride safe and intact.

"I'll stay away. From now on, sweetheart, you're on your own. The offer will remain to buy the place. When you're tired of playing at ranching, let Richard know and we can finalize the deal."

Trace walked by her, his boots loud in the sudden silence. He retrieved his hat and let himself out the back door. Kalli sat still, feeling her insides dissolve. She wanted him to stay. Wanted him to finish the dinner he'd been fixing her. Wanted his help. Wanted his bossy orders. Wanted more of his kisses.

A shiver of fear touched her. She had overestimated her ability. Uncle Philip had made it seem so easy, but she didn't have the faintest idea how to run a ranch. She didn't know how to manage cattle. Didn't understand the information she'd been putting into the computer. How could she make sense of it? She couldn't stay on a horse, couldn't even saddle one without help. How could she manage on her own?

She needed Trace.

And he knew it. Without his help, she would probably wreck the ranch in record time. Well, that would make it all the easier for him to buy it.

She pushed herself up and hurried to the door, hopping, unable to keep her injured foot from touching every few steps. Pain shot up her leg, but she ignored it. Throwing open the wooden door, she pushed through the screen door and out onto the porch.

"Trace!"

He was already in his truck, the engine on. For a long moment the air vibrated with the throaty growl of the big pickup. Then he shut it off and the silence was deafening.

Blood pounded through her, roaring in her ears as she strained to see him in the darkness. To her left the soft glow of lights from the bunkhouse illuminated a portion of the yard. Behind her the light from the kitchen shone, but beyond that, there was only darkness. She tried to see him, but could only hear the truck door open, close. Could only hear the crunch of gravel beneath his boots as he walked closer.

"What?"

He came into the circle of light spilling from the doorway and stood looking at her. His hat rode low on his forehead, his legs spread in an arrogant stance as he glared at her. She stood two steps higher, making her a shade taller than he was.

Kalli licked her lips. "I'm sorry. Please, I'm sorry. Try to understand this from my point of view. I've wanted to live on the ranch since I was a child, since my first visit. All my life I've longed for this. To be given this chance, it's as if a dream came true. Haven't you ever had a dream? A wonderful dream that is so special you can't believe it when it comes true?"

He stared at her, his lips tight, his eyes narrowed as he watched her try to explain to him.

"I know I don't know anything about ranching, but I'm willing to learn. You're not willing to give me the chance, however. Every time I do anything, I run into a solid wall of your disapproval and dislike."

"I told you before, I don't dislike you," he said, his voice hard, cold.

"Maybe physically. But otherwise you don't want me here. You said so again just minutes ago. But let me tell you that I'm staying. I'm here for good. If I have to end up shooting my cattle one by one to eat to live, I'm staying. If I have to get a pony to ride because I can't saddle a big horse, I'll do it. If I have to invent my own system of record keeping because I can't figure out that blasted computer, I'll do it. But I'm here for the long haul."

She took a deep breath, her eyes fixed on his.

"I want you to help me. Give me a chance. A real chance. Please, Trace. I know it is not to your best advantage, but please give me a chance. Teach me what I need to know. Let me have a fair shot at staying."

"You can stay, you don't need me."

"I do, to make a go of it. Please, Trace, I'll give you anything you want, except the ranch. Help me."

"And if the price is too high?" he said.

He was going to do it. He was going to help her!

"It won't be."

"What if I want you?"

She smiled, the warm glow of his words caressing her. Slowly she reached out her hand and trailed her fingers down his cheek, feeling a muscle jump beneath her touch.

"Silly, I know you want me. You've made that clear all along. You keep saying it has nothing to do with the ranch."

"And?"

Kalli swallowed hard. "And I want you. I wasn't handing you a line earlier, this morning was very special to me. I get hot and excited just thinking about it."

"Hell." He reached out and pulled her off-balance, crashing against him. His arms tightened around her until he could feel the soft mounds of her breasts pressing intimately against his chest, could feel the heat of her belly against his, the smooth strength of her thighs matching his. Burying his face in the strawberry fragrance of her hair, he held her tightly, letting himself feel the feminine mystery and magic of her soothe him, inflame him. God, he wanted her!

Kalli remained silent, reveling in the sensations that wrapped around her. She pressed against him, feeling the solid wall of rock-hard muscles shelter her. Closing her eyes, she breathed in his scent and grew warm and languid with desire. She pressed her lips against his neck, trailed them to the pulse point at the base of his throat and let them lie against his steady beat. Daringly her tongue darted out and tasted him. She felt him tighten against her, felt the growing arousal that assured her he wanted her as much as she wanted him.

Smiling in shy satisfaction, she kissed him again.

With a groan, he tipped back her head and captured her lips with his own. Flames of desire licked between them as they strained to get closer. His mouth opened hers, and when his tongue began its explorations, she met him, enticed him, tantalized him.

Shifting slightly, Kalli put weight on her injured foot and the pain spiked through her. She moaned involuntarily, shifting away from it.

Trace pulled back, his eyes puzzled for a moment, then reality intruded.

"Dumb move on my part." He lifted her again and headed for the lighted room beyond the screen door. Depositing her in a chair, he sat back on his haunches and stared at her, one hand gently brushing away the strands of hair that fell across her face.

"Don't stop," she whispered, her palm caressing his cheek, feeling the end-of-day stubble rasp against her skin. "I don't need that foot anyway." She leaned forward and brushed his lips with her own.

"You're battered and bruised and have a sprained ankle. And you're hungry, or so you said," he answered, rising. He hung his hat on the rack and turned to the counter.

She frowned. "I don't want to stop," she said, watching him. Why had he stopped?

"Honey, when you and I come together, it's going to be wild and hot and hard and I don't want to have to pull back for fear of hurting you. We can wait. After all, didn't you just insist you're here for the long haul?'' His voice had a hard edge to it.

She nodded. What a complex man. She was sure he'd take her right to bed, love her until morning. Now he appeared to be willing to wait. Her gaze dropped to his jeans. Men couldn't hide desire. His control must be formidable. Why wouldn't he just take what she was so willing to offer?

She closed her eyes, sizzling with memories of that morning. Remembering what he just said. When they got together it would be hot and hard and wild. Her heart raced. Just being with him was wild. What would making love be like?

"So you will help me learn how to ranch?'' she asked.

He gave a lopsided smile. "How to ranch. Hell, I guess so. You won't last.''

"Stop it! I don't want to hear it. You may be right, but that doesn't mean I want to hear it all the time. Besides, if you don't help me, I'll sell somewhere else if I can't make it myself,'' she said dangerously.

"Oh, yeah? No one else has made an offer that I heard of,'' he replied easily.

He wasn't worried. The only other property that might ever want her land was the Bar M Ranch, which touched the corner of her land near the river. And Bob Marshall had never voiced any desire to expand his place. Trace wasn't worried. Sooner or later the lady from Boston would admit she was not a rancher, and hightail it right back to the big city where she belonged.

What worried him was his reaction to her personally. Very personally. He wanted her like he'd never wanted anyone. Even Alyssa's sexual attraction when he had been a randy young rodeo cowboy didn't begin to compare to Kalli Bonotelli's. He didn't understand it. Was it just celibacy that drove him? It had been a long time, but he'd gone long stretches of time without a woman be-

fore and never felt this ... this *craving*. He knew it had
nothing to do with wanting her land. If she signed everything over to him today, he'd still want her in bed.

He didn't like it. Didn't like feeling so caught up with
his emotions that he almost lost control. And that was the
reason he held off tonight. Just to prove to himself he
could. He was in charge of this. When he deemed the
time right, he would take her to bed. But he was not giving in to his instincts or her pretty, pouting mouth. He'd
choose the time and place.

"Glaring at the eggs won't cook them," she said softly,
the teasing lilt in her voice jerking him to awareness.

He stared at her over those high sculpted cheeks, his
look cold and hard. "Never bite the hand that feeds
you."

She smiled slowly, seductively, and shook her head. "I
never would," she said in a low voice, her gaze holding
his. "I might nibble a bit. Even nibble elsewhere ..."

He sucked in his breath at the image that danced before him, of her sprawled across his bed, her mouth on
him hot and sexy. Maybe the time and place was now and
here after all.

She laughed at his reaction, pleased beyond anything
she was able to invoke a reaction. Maybe he wasn't as
immune to her as she thought when he pushed her away.
Maybe he did want to wait until she was healed, the better to love her. She was thrilled. Gingerly she rotated her
foot, unable to keep the grimace of pain away. Damn, she
wanted to heal fast, to see what this cowboy had in mind
for the two of them.

In the meantime, she would spend her time learning
everything she could about running a ranch.

The omelet was light and delicious. He found an old
bottle of wine and they shared it as Kalli complimented
him on her dinner.

"Didn't know you were so talented," she said when she pushed her empty plate away. "That beats whatever Charlie would have brought."

"Charlie's a good cook."

"So I hear. But that was wonderful. Do you cook at home?"

"No. I have a housekeeper, Betty. She cooks, stays over when I need someone to be there with Becky."

"Is she young and pretty?" Kalli asked, toying with her wineglass, sloshing the pale liquid around and around. Almost holding her breath for his reply.

He chuckled, stretched back in the chair, his long legs crossed at the ankles. Tucking his thumbs in his belt, he shrugged. "I reckon her husband, Ed, thinks she's pretty. As to age, she's about fifty. Where is that on your old-to-young scale?"

"Let me see, if a rodeo cowboy is old at thirty-four..."

"Witch," he said without heat.

She laughed and flirted with him. Squeezing every moment of enjoyment from the evening. Daringly she rose on her good leg and hopped over to him, plopping herself down on his lap. His surprise enchanted her as he sat up, drew in his legs to hold her, his arms going around her so she wouldn't fall.

"What the hell—"

"I want you to kiss me," she said, putting her arms around his neck, snuggling against him, her breasts pressing against him.

"Kalli, no. I told you—"

"Just a kiss, Trace, nothing more."

God, nothing more? One touch of that sweet mouth and he would be all over her like flies on honey. No matter what his intentions, no matter how much control he thought he had, there were limits.

"Kalli."

"Just a few kisses, Trace. Then I'll go to bed like a good little girl. A chaste little girl, if you prefer." She chuckled and kissed his jaw. Trailing her open mouth across the stubble of his beard, she tasted him with her tongue.

He moved to intercept her lips with his, locking her into an embrace that seared them both. One hand scooped her bottom to hold her higher against his chest while the other threaded through her soft hair, holding her for his kiss. His tongue tormented her, delving deep within the warm sweetness of her mouth to taste every part of her, tasting the wine and Kalli's own unique flavor. Her lips moved against his as she met his every thrust with wild abandon, returned every stroke of pleasure with one of her own.

She was breathing so hard she thought she might pass out. But she couldn't get enough of Trace. She cursed the clothing that stood between them, cursed his decision to wait until she was better. She was so hot she could hardly stand it. She longed to expose her skin to his, feel his heat wrap around her and take her away from the mundane chores of running a ranch, no matter how much she wanted it.

"Enough." He pulled away, still holding her hard against him, his hot breath spilling over her shoulder.

Idly Kalli noted he was breathing as erratically as she. Good, she didn't want to be the only one effected by that kiss. She felt as if she would melt into a tiny puddle. Slowly her breathing steadied. Her awareness returned, and with it a nagging pain.

"Trace, you're pulling my hair," she whispered, unable to move.

Slowly he released his grip on her silky hair, soothing her scalp. "Sorry. But I had to hold on to something or strip this little T-shirt off you, put you on the table and take you right here. I told you we'll wait!"

"You're always telling me things. Why not explain so I understand, rather than just order me around," she said, pulling away enough to look into his eyes.

He stared at her. "I've been boss for so long, I'm not used to explaining things."

"Even physicians explain why they are prescribing treatments for patients to their lowly nurses. If you would give me reasons, maybe I wouldn't react so strongly to your bossy ways."

"So giving you reasons will stop your arguing at every pass?"

"Now, I didn't promise that, exactly. But it would go a long ways toward better harmony between us."

"I think the harmony between us is just fine." He caressed her hip lightly with his roughened hand.

"Stop that or I'll never get to sleep."

"Which is what you need." With no effort he rose and carried her into her bedroom. "Will you be all right during the night?"

"If you're worried about me, you could stay," she said, drawing the sheet over herself, trying to see his expression in the dim light spilling in from the hall. He hadn't put on her light.

"Not on your life. What would my daughter think?" he asked.

"Isn't she asleep by now?"

"Yeah, and has been for hours. It's after midnight, sweetheart, give me a break. I need some rest before tomorrow."

"And you wouldn't get it here?" she asked in mock disbelief, shivering in delight at teasing him.

"No, and you know it. I'll be back for breakfast."

"Charlie—"

"Dammit, Kalli, leave it. I said I'll take care of you and I will."

"What are you, top dog and I'm your bone? Fine. Come by in the morning." Why was he so insistent about taking care of her? Didn't she have cowboys she could ask to help?

"Kalli, you know I still want your ranch?" His voice was low, his tone serious.

"I thought you weren't going to bring that up all the time."

"I'm not. I'm not going to say anything about it again. But I want you to know that I want the land. No matter what happens, don't go thinking anything is going on that's not. Sooner or later, I'll have the Triple T."

"Give it up, Trace."

"Just so you know."

"I know. What's the matter, are you afraid I'll take this thing between us too seriously, that I might think you're falling for me? Or me for you?"

"I'm immune, but are you?"

"You think I'm some starry-eyed young girl who's going to fall head over heels in love with the first cowboy that comes along, don't you?" Her heart was racing now. It had nothing to do with him. He was attractive. He was appealing. He made her feel sensations she'd never even known existed before. But she would not let herself fall in love with a man who distrusted women as much as he did. She would not!

"Yeah. What have you done to show me any different? Are you going to tell me you have love affairs all the time?"

Love affairs? Did he see this as a love affair? The man who didn't believe in love? Her heart beat harder, so hard he had to see it. She could fall for this man so easily. If she could get past the hurt of his wanting her to leave. If she could only get him to see her for herself and not as a representative of a betraying female who had left him alone with a young baby and never looked back.

"No, I don't. Are you kidding, with five brothers?"

"You didn't live at home, surely you could be discreet."

"Go away, Trace. This conversation is getting more personal than I want. I may not be as accomplished in that area as you, but I'm not a virgin, if that's what's worrying you."

He was intrigued. She was from Boston, a decade out of high school. Surely she'd had some affairs. What had the men been like? Had they satisfied her? Was she still looking for love like in some fairy tale, or was she on the make for a likely meal ticket? The man with the most money wins?

"I never thought you were a virgin, Not the way you kiss."

She was pleased. At least she did something right.

"Want another one before you go?"

"Yeah, only then I wouldn't be going. Good night, Kalli. Hope you sleep well."

"Thanks. You, too."

Yeah, right. He had as much chance of sleeping as she did of running a marathon tomorrow. He was tired, but his mind was too full of her to relax, to sleep. He'd scarcely get home before it would be time to get up. It was going to be a long night.

Seven

It was midmorning when Trace drove into Kalli's yard and drew to a stop beside the kitchen door. He had taken care of a few things at his own place, letting Kalli sleep in. When he opened the screen door to the kitchen, he was startled to see her standing by the sink, washing dishes. She was balanced on a pair of old crutches, her long legs bare and tanned beneath an indecently skimpy pair of white shorts. Her yellow cotton shirt was fitted, showing every delectable curve even more than the T-shirts she slept in. He stopped dead, staring at her.

She turned and smiled at him. Her eyes were bright and sparkling, her dark hair tied back in a thick ponytail.

"You must have slept in," she said.

"I thought I'd leave that to you. How long have you been up?"

"For ages. Charlie came by to check on me, but I was already up and dressed, so get that scowl off your face. He found these crutches for me. Apparently some cowboy a few years back broke his leg and used them. They had to be adjusted for me, of course.''

Her sunny smile warmed him. He stood in the doorway and watched her talk, watched the animation in her face. Except for the evidence of the crutches and the bandage around her ankle, she looked as fresh and fine as anyone he'd ever seen.

Tossing his hat on the rack, he crossed the floor to pour himself a cup of coffee. He leaned against the counter while he sipped.

"So you ate?''

"Yes, just finishing cleaning up. What do you have planned to teach me today?''

"The ranch is late in its spring roundup. We'll discuss that." He took a sip of the hot coffee, his eyes drawn again to her shapely legs. He remembered how silky her skin had felt beneath his fingers, how he'd like to feel those tanned legs wrapped around him, holding him tightly against her. Closing his eyes, he forced himself to look away, think about the work yet to be done.

"Shall we use the office?'' she asked brightly, a flood of sensations shimmering at his look. She licked her lips, wishing he'd kissed her good morning. Wishing for a lot of things that had nothing to do with learning to run a ranch.

"Yeah, the office is fine.'' Without waiting for her, he pushed away from the counter and headed down the hall.

By the time Kalli reached the room her uncle had used as the ranch office, Trace was sitting behind the desk, looking at her stacks of bills and reports on the desk.

"How far along are you?''

"I'm up to April,'' she replied, sinking into one of the comfortable chairs across from the desk. Pushing the other one around, she rested her injured ankle on it.

"How's the ankle?'' he asked, still studying the piles she'd made when organizing all the material for input-

ting into the computer, afraid if he looked at those silky
legs again he'd forget why he'd come.

"Better. With the crutches I'm more mobile and yet
can keep off it."

He swiveled around in the chair, leaned back and
studied her, careful to keep his gaze on her face.

"So tell me all I need to know about spring roundup,"
she said as the silence stretched out.

"It's hot, dirty, hard work. You have two choices, take
it easy and have it last for several days, or go full out and
get it over with as quickly as possible."

"Which do you recommend?" she asked.

"On my place I do it as quickly as possible. But it
means getting up before dawn and usually not stopping
until it's too dark to see."

"Doing it that way, how long does it take?"

"At Flying Cloud? A week or longer. It's a bigger
spread than yours. Here, it would only take a few days.
But you need a bigger crew."

"You mean hire some more cowboys?"

"Yeah. Or get neighbors to help. Usually the ranches
around here stagger their roundups so they can help each
other out. Then there are always drifters looking for a
short job before moving on to the next place."

"I don't know any neighbors, except you."

"But they all know the Triple T, and most of them
have probably heard all about you by now. You want to
ask for their help?"

"And I help in return when they need it?"

He nodded. "You and your men when they ask."

"Okay, if you think that'll work. I can start calling today. Who should I call?"

He started to say he'd take care of it. That he'd take
care of everything for her, but hesitated. She wanted to
run this place by herself, now was as good a time as any

for her to start. To learn all that was entailed, and how complex and difficult it really was.

"I'll make you a list of the men you should talk to. Tell them I said to call." He drew out a tablet and began writing names.

"If I didn't mention you, would I get the same response?" she asked suspiciously.

"Probably not." He looked up, back to the writing. "There isn't another female rancher in these parts. Most of the men are a little chauvinistic in their outlook."

"No, really?" She grinned. She had been around the most chauvinistic man she'd ever seen for days. How could she not suspect everyone around here was like that?

"You have a problem with that?" His eyes narrowed as he looked up.

"I'm not used to it." Actually the thought of Trace taking care of her was appealing—to a degree. But she was an independent woman. She might like to rely on someone, but only to the extent they also relied on her.

"Here's the list. Pick a date, start calling. Get as many men lined up as you can. When you know how many are coming, you have to plan the logistics of the roundup. Where are you going to hold it, how are you going to get food and drinks to the men, what about feed for the horses? Will you provide a place for them to sleep, or expect them to return to their ranches each night? Depending on the distance, that will cut into the workday."

"Wait a minute, I need to get all this down on paper." She drew the tablet across and began to make notes.

Trace spent the remainder of the morning going over every aspect with her, explaining when she had questions, making suggestions when she seemed totally lost. A couple of times he gave an order and then quickly took it back when she glared at him. By the time he rose to leave, she had a million things to do to plan her first roundup. The tasks seemed insurmountable, and this was only one aspect of a busy ranch. She took a deep breath. She would take it one step at a time.

"Want to stay for lunch?" she offered as he reached the door.

"No, got to get back to my own place before it falls into rack and ruin."

She doubted it had suffered at all in the time he'd been here. She bet every one of the men on his place knew his own job and did it well without supervision. Trace wouldn't put up with any slackers.

That afternoon Kalli began calling her neighbors, introducing herself on the phone and asking for their help. As the day waned, she didn't know whether to be amused or annoyed. She was certainly exasperated with the common theme of all the calls. "Thought Trace was buying that place," was the most common comment. "Trace can handle it," was the second most common. But once everyone heard he'd told her to call, they quickly agreed to help. She wondered what the outcome would have been if Trace had not been on her side.

He was doing more for her than she'd realized. It would have been much easier, and more to his benefit, to ignore her, let her flounder around on her own. She might have ended up eating her own cattle to survive, just as she'd threatened.

Kalli made her way to the bunkhouse for dinner. Charlie had prepared a delicious stew and she enjoyed the camaraderie of the men as they shared dinner. She soaked up the tales they told of past hardships and glories. She asked questions. She discovered Charlie had been a Marine for a while, José was courting a girl in Jackson and Tim still had dreams of winning some rodeo title. The men seemed equally fascinated by her stories. The cosmopolitan city of Boston was as far removed from what they were used to as Paris or London would have been.

And she asked copious questions about the ranch every chance she got. Charlie and Josh had been there the longest, over ten years, coming just after her last visit. They answered every question she asked, volunteered things she hadn't thought about. From their quiet, differential manner, she knew they were a little wary of her being able to run the place, but they were willing to go along for the time being and give her a chance. It made her feel welcomed for the first time since arriving in Wyoming.

As Kalli prepared for bed, she reflected on the day. It had been great. Except she missed Trace after he left. He hadn't even touched her today. After last night, she thought he'd be a little more amorous. The kisses they'd shared had almost been X-rated. The feelings he built in her were so *erotic* she could scarcely stand to be apart from him. He could have at least kissed her.

The phone rang. She sank on the bed and picked it up.

"Kalli?"

"Trace, I was just thinking about you."

"Yeah, me, too. You okay?"

"Sure. I'm in bed now."

He was silent, picturing her in bed. He wanted to be there with her.

"Trace?" she said softly as the silence dragged on.

"Yeah?"

"Did you call for a reason?"

"Just to see how you are doing. How's your ankle?"

"It's feeling better. Still sore if I put any weight on it." Remembering what she'd been thinking about, she decided to test the waters. She felt safe with him several miles away. Worst case, she could always hang up on him.

"Actually, I have other parts that ache a bit more." She lay back against her pillows, smiling into the phone, her voice low and husky.

"Where, your shoulder?"

"No, my lips. My...breasts. Do you know anyone who could kiss and make them better?" Her voice teased, craved, tantalized.

"Oh, God," he groaned. "Hell, Kalli, why don't you just walk naked in front of me?"

"Would that work?" she asked, smiling in quiet satisfaction. Maybe he did still want her, though he had a funny way of showing it by ignoring her today.

"I'll come over and we'll see." The hard edge in his tone denied the romantic overtones she longed to hear.

"Don't you dare. I'm all ready to go to sleep. My whole body feels as if it lost out to a steamroller. My ankle really does hurt. I need to get better before..."

"Before?"

"You know."

He chuckled. "Maybe you better tell me."

"Trace, you're a rancher, you figure it out."

"Meaning?"

"You've got cows and bulls and stallions and mares."

"Honey, what's between us is more than what's between animals in heat."

She felt warmth spread through every cell.

"You're right," she whispered. She didn't just want a physical relationship with him. She wanted more. She liked arguing with him about the ranch. Liked pitting her wits against his. Liked listening to him talk, share the vast knowledge he had of ranching and cattle and handling men. She wanted to spend more time with him doing whatever he wanted. Riding, fixing fences or sitting on the porch and enjoying the breeze from the mountains. She wanted more than just a roll in the hay with this cowboy. Lots more. And as far into the future as she could see, she didn't have much chance.

"Damn straight, I am. Go to sleep," he growled.

* * *

Trace hung up the phone and moved to the window, staring out across the darkness to where he knew her house sat. He couldn't stop thinking about her. And her provocative conversation wasn't helping. He couldn't deny the ache that he carried around all the time, wanting her. He wasn't used to women like her. She had been delighted, positively sparkling when they discussed the roundup. She hadn't been overwhelmed by all the details that needed attention. She hadn't been cowed by the work involved. She'd plunged right in. Happy.

He'd heard from Bob Marshall and Tom Hyden already. They were sending men to the roundup, both coming themselves, just to meet the new neighbor and see if she was as dainty as the bank president had said.

They sounded pleased with Kalli. For a moment he frowned. He didn't want other men around her. He didn't want her fitting into the community, making friends. Didn't want her doing anything that was going to make it harder for her to leave. She was so stubborn already, any slight foothold would only strengthen her resolve to remain.

He leaned his arm against the window frame and leaned closer to the glass, seeing his reflection, seeing it fade as his imagination pictured her in bed, with one of those soft T-shirts she wore. Her legs would be bare. She'd have taken off her panties. Her dark silky hair would be spread out over the white pillowcase, soft and wavy. He clenched his hand into a fist, trying to erase the feel of her hair from his fingertips. She'd been so responsive last night, despite her injuries. God, when she'd been beneath him in her bed that morning it had taken all his control to keep from ripping off his jeans and plunging into her wet heat.

She was so pretty. All over. Her hair was always clean and glossy and smelled slightly of strawberries. He loved the feel of it against his rough hands. He wondered why he'd ever liked blondes. Her sparkling eyes were always laughing. Well, almost always. Other times they were snapping in anger at him. Or soft as a velvet night in summer when he was kissing her. And she packed more passion in that little body of hers than anyone he'd ever met.

Even Alyssa.

Hell, he didn't want to think about Alyssa. *But he should.* He kept her picture by his bed to remind him every day. He needed to remember how crazy he'd been for her, almost as crazy as he felt around Kalli. Crazy enough to marry her. But it had proved a major disaster. She'd left, abandoning him and their daughter. Taking all the money they'd saved to expand the ranch. Leaving her husband and baby to struggle for years to bring the ranch around. And she'd been more used to ranches and cowboys and the kind of life he led than Kalli. Starry-eyed, optimistic Kalli who wanted to live on a ranch, but didn't have a clue to what all that entailed. No, he better not forget Alyssa and the lesson she'd taught him. Turning away in disgust, he prepared for bed.

When Kalli awoke the next morning she felt better. Except for the ache in her ankle and the bruise on her shoulder, she felt normal. The stiffness from riding had disappeared. The aches from her fall had faded. She continued to use the crutches, to give her ankle the best care she could. But she was on the mend. Fixing herself breakfast, she noticed Trace's truck was parked in its usual spot. He hadn't stopped in to see her, however. Had he come early, when she'd still been asleep? Surely he'd stop in before he left for home. She'd see him then.

Impatient with being stuck inside on such a beautiful day, Kalli nevertheless headed for the office once breakfast was behind her. She wanted to be caught up on the blasted records so she could turn to other activities. Her ankle provided the perfect excuse to finish the computer work. Once she was fit again, she wanted to be out doing things, not stuck in the office. And once Trace showed her how to run reports and what they meant, she'd be that much closer to being a true rancher.

She hoped once everything was input that it wouldn't take long to do the chore each week. She understood how important it was from a business point of view to keep records up to date. She had always been meticulous with her patients' records. But bookkeeping just wasn't fun for her. She'd much rather be with people.

Early afternoon saw her through April. She only had the current month's bills, records and payments to do and she would be caught up. Stretching, she winced slightly when her sore shoulder protested, then eased back in the chair. Time for a break.

Wandering out on the porch, she gazed off across the fields toward the mountains. Would she ever get tired of the view? The slight breeze seemed to come straight from the highest peak, carrying with it the fresh scent of snow and grass and clean air. Quite a change from Boston.

When she was feeling better, and the ranch was running smoothly, she'd like to take a short trip to Yellowstone, see more of the countryside. She sighed, wishing Trace would offer to take her. But knowing him, he probably didn't do anything that wasn't related to his ranch. Did he ever have fun?

She spotted Becky on her horse coming up the drive. Smiling, she called a greeting.

"Hi, what brings you this way?"

"Hi, Kalli. I'm looking for Dad again. Is he here?"

"No, his truck's been here since this morning, but I haven't seen him or any of the men all day. Come in and visit awhile."

Becky hesitated, then nodded. "I'll leave my horse by the corral."

Kalli watched as the girl competently dismounted and loosened the girth on the saddle. She made sure her horse had some water, then tied him in the shade of the big barn.

"I was just taking a break," Kalli said as Becky joined her on the porch.

"From what? What can you do with a busted ankle?"

"It's only sprained, thank goodness. And I've been a slave to the computer all morning. I feel as if my mind is one big number."

"Dad has a computer."

"Does he use it all the time?"

"A lot. Most nights he does some work on it. That way it doesn't all pile up," she said, as if she was quoting her father.

"Well, I wished he'd done more about keeping up this one. Not that it was his place," Kalli said quickly at the look Becky gave her. "But it would have been a help to me. I don't know much about computers to begin with, and having to spend hours every day with them is not why I came to Wyoming."

"Why did you come? Just to see the ranch?"

"Yes. And to live here. I love it."

"It's early yet, you won't like it for long."

"I think I will. I used to visit it when I was a teenager. I've always loved it."

"My mom was from Colorado, used to ranches and everything, and she left. Dad said she thought it was too...too something that means out in the boonies."

"Isolated?"

"Yeah, I guess."

"Do you find it isolated?" Kalli asked.

"No, I like it."

"Are you still in school?"

"Naw, we're out for the summer."

"So what do you do for fun?"

"Ride, swim, help my dad. He's teaching me how to be a rancher. I'll own the Flying Cloud Ranch someday," she said.

"What if he marries again, and has more kids. Wouldn't you have to share?"

Becky shrugged. "I don't guess he'll ever marry. My mom's been gone since I was a baby and I'm almost grown."

Kalli hid a smile, trying to remember back to when she was twelve. It seemed so long ago. Yet she remembered feeling quite grown-up.

"He might find someone someday and marry."

"I asked him once, but he said he didn't need a wife, that things were just fine the way they were. Once, when I was a kid, I wanted a mother. I'm the only one in my class that doesn't have one. Or one that lives with us, I guess I mean."

"Trace said you don't see your mother."

"Naw, she didn't want to be bothered with me."

Kalli didn't know what to say. She didn't know enough about what had actually happened to offer platitudes to Becky. And she wasn't one to cover up. Life was hard, and Becky seemed well-adjusted despite not having a mother.

"So when you were a kid you wanted a mother, but not now?"

Becky shrugged. "I don't know. Might be nice. Someone to go shopping with besides Dad. He doesn't like looking at clothes or records or things like that."

Kalli smiled. "I imagine your father is a difficult man to go shopping with. He probably has a list and walks right over to what he has on the list and buys it, then leaves."

Becky glanced at her and smiled, nodding. "Exactly."

"My brothers are like that. Whereas we women know the best way to shop is to examine everything, then we can select exactly the right item. And sometimes it's fun just to browse. I know my mother and I love to shop. There's this place in Boston, called Filen's, where you can get the best bargains. We'll spend hours there and sometimes not even buy a single thing. But it's fun. We talk and visit and get away from the men. Did you know I have five brothers?"

"Wow. How did you stand it?"

"They're great. You can meet them when they come to visit me."

"If you stay that long," Becky said.

"Now you sound like your father. Want to make some brownies?"

"What?"

"We can make some brownies. I'm hungry for something chocolate, and it's more fun to do things together with someone."

Becky hesitated, looking away. "I've never made brownies," she said finally.

"Well, you won't learn any younger. In fact, you can do most of the work, since I'm almost an invalid."

"I'm sorry you got hurt," Becky said slowly.

"No big deal. If I can't manage a horse, maybe I'll buy a pony."

Becky giggled. "Ranchers don't ride ponies."

"Your father had a slightly glazed look when I told him, as well. I guess that means I'll have to master horsemanship. Come on and let's make brownies."

Deciding it would be selfish for them to make brownies only for themselves, they made two big batches, one for them to eat and the second batch for the men when they came in.

Kalli enjoyed the afternoon. Becky was a mixture of shyness and bold opinions. Many of the opinions directly reflected those of her father. Kalli laughed out loud a couple of times when Becky reminded her strongly of Trace. It seemed odd to hear his words from a girl.

Becky was taking the final batch from the oven when Trace walked in. The kitchen was a mess. Several bowls were lined up on the counter, racks of cooling brownies jockeyed for space on the table, and flour, sugar and chocolate dotted everything. Kalli sat in a chair, her injured ankle resting on the seat of another, directing Becky.

"Something smells good." Trace stared at Kalli, questioning.

"I made brownies, Dad!" Becky said excitedly. "Do you want one?"

"Sure do. I didn't know you knew how to make them." He took a large one from the plate and bit into it, his eyes drawn to Kalli.

"I didn't before now. Kalli showed me how."

"Want some milk to go with it?" Kalli asked, sitting up a little straighter. Suddenly she felt exhilarated, the pleasure of the afternoon magnified by his presence.

"I'll get it." Becky put the pan of brownies down and went to the refrigerator.

"Get some for us, as well. We'll join your father."

"You haven't had any yet?" Trace asked, sitting next to Kalli. He let his eyes roam over her, noticing the quickened breathing, the long legs in shorts again. He looked away. He'd be glad when she was back to jeans. Closing his eyes briefly, he remembered how she'd filled out the denim. Maybe it wouldn't be an improvement for his equilibrium, after all. Damn!

"Well, we did sample a couple, just to make sure they weren't poison," Kalli said slowly, her eyes twinkling.

Becky giggled, placed glasses on the table and poured the milk.

"Kalli knows how to cook and said she'd teach me," Becky said, sitting happily beside her father and reaching for a brownie.

"Oh, so you can cook as well as nurse?"

"Sure. My mother made sure all of us knew how to cook. Though I have to tell you I don't do much on my own. And mostly I know how to cook for a crowd. With all of us at home, you learn to prepare a lot of food. Then we always had company. A couple of my brothers had best friends that we thought we had adopted, they were over so much."

"And did you have friends over, too?" Trace asked, watching her talk about her home and family, enchanted with the sparkling happiness reflected in her expression. He'd like to see her in her parents' home. Would have liked to see her as a little girl.

"Sure, but not at every meal. And not if I was cooking. Then I wanted as few people over as possible."

"What's your specialty?"

"Anything Italian, what else? Mama always had the best pasta. She made it herself, you see. Then we learned how to make all the rich sauces that curl your toes, they're so good. Daddy would always judge our efforts, and proclaim Mama the winner."

"Sounds as if you have a close family," Trace said.

"We are. We get together every month, the whole crew, and eat and talk and visit. It's fun."

"You'll miss it."

"Well, yes, I will. But they can come to visit. After all, it isn't as if I had still been living at home. And my brothers all have their own lives, as well."

"Still, Wyoming is a long way from Boston."

Kalli narrowed her gaze. "Forget it, Trace. I have a phone and we can write letters. I can go visit once a year and they can come here. It's not that far. I'm—"

"Here to stay," he chanted with her.

She laughed. "Do you like the brownies?"

"They're very good. You did a good job, Becky."

"Thanks, Dad."

"Your family's pretty close, too, Trace," she said softly. She liked the relationship between them. It was warm and loving. While Becky might miss her mother, she had not lacked for love from her father. She clearly adored him.

"We're all each other has," Trace said with a warm smile at his daughter.

Kalli felt a twinge of jealousy. She didn't like the fact, but there it was. She wished he'd consider including her in their warm, close family. Shocked at where her thoughts were leading, she took a hasty sip of milk. Granted, she felt around Trace than any man she'd known, but she couldn't be falling in love with him. He'd made it so clear he wasn't interested. He saw her only as the obstacle to be overcome to acquire the ranch.

She held still, hoping the feeling would fade. It didn't. It grew stronger and stronger until she felt swamped, overwhelmed. Her heart almost burst. She loved him! He was dead set against her and she loved him. Oh, God, how had that happened? When had it happened? She flicked a quick glance at him, afraid it would show in her face. The last thing she dared do was let him know. He'd laugh her all the way back to Boston. She had been so sure she could control her emotions. Sure she could have a wild affair with a cocky cowboy, then continue blithely along her merry way. Now she wanted more.

She wanted him to love her. She wanted him to ask her to stay, to forget about her ranch and his belief she wouldn't fit in. She wanted him to love her back.

Stunned at the churning thoughts that spun around and around, she was almost unaware when Trace ordered Becky to clean up and asked to see Kalli in the office.

Rising slowly, she led the way, conscious of him only inches behind her. Conscious of his height towering over her, of his strong arms and shoulders that had carried her effortlessly several times. Conscious of his stern look and determined goals. Warmed by his fierce love for his daughter. Loving everything about him.

Closing the study door behind him, he reached out and pulled her into his arms without a word. His kiss was magic. Kalli dropped the crutches, ignoring their clatter as she wound her arms around his neck and moved as close as she could for the ecstasy of his kiss.

"If I call you tonight," he said, his lips moving against hers, "I want a clear yes or no to my questions."

His tongue swept into her mouth, claiming her for himself. Learning her, tasting her, mating with her tongue. When she accepted his invitation and pushed her tongue into his mouth, he felt the heat flood through him. He wanted her. Damnation, how he wanted this little slip of a woman.

He broke the kiss, moving back an inch, but keeping her against him so tightly not even a breath of air could separate them. "None of that bit about other parts of you hurting. I'll kiss them better now, and that'll have to carry you over, understand?"

She nodded, lost in the bliss of his caresses, his teasing tone seeping through her like fine wine. It was fun to be part of a couple, fun to tease and be teased. One arm held her up while the other came around and slipped between them. His fingers sought the buttons on her shirt, released them slowly one by one. His mouth continued to merge with hers, his lips doing wonderful things as she reveled in the sexy, sensual sensations that poured through her. She could no longer think, only feel. Feel the love she had for this man swell in her as his embrace captivated her.

When her shirt was unfastened, he spread it wide and traced kisses down her throat, across the delicate bones of her shoulders, down, down until he captured a rosy tip through the lacy bra. He wet it, blew on it, pulled it into his mouth.

Kalli floated on a sea of sensuality, his mouth fanning the fire between them. Every suckling action drew her deeper into the flame, every nerve ending tingled in longing, every fiber of her being craved closer contact.

Her hands scrambled for his buttons, frantically ripping them apart in her haste to feel his taut muscles against her bare skin. Her fingers trailed across the strong muscles of his chest, finding and savoring the feel of his hard, tight nipples.

When he unfastened her bra, she shrugged it and her shirt off, moving back to his embrace. Closing her eyes in delight at the feel of his hard chest against her swollen breasts, her mouth sought his. She sighed in soft satisfaction when he met her lips with his own and kissed her long and hard.

His roughened hands rubbed along the soft skin of her back, sending shivers of pleasure racing through her. He was so hot and hard. She shimmered with the thought of him crushing her beneath him, mastering her with his love and taking her through the spinning vortex that threatened to consume her.

"Dad? I'm finished," Becky called from the kitchen.

Trace spun Kalli around, pressing her against the door, holding her as he held the door closed against his daughter.

"I've a few things to finish up here, punkin. Why don't you get started for home and I'll catch up in the truck." He was breathing hard, making every effort to have his words sound normal. Perspiration glistened on his forehead.

Kalli stared at him, her eyes glittering with desire and yearning, her body relishing the feel of his weight against it as he pressed her into the cool wood. The danger of discovery by Becky only heightened her awareness of their situation. His skin was hot, damp, slick against hers. His weight held her against the door, the pain in her ankle forgotten.

"Okay. Bye, Kalli, thanks for teaching me to make brownies."

It was her turn. She cleared her throat. "We'll do it again soon." Surely she didn't sound that weak.

They didn't move, standing still as statues. Kalli held her breath, straining to hear Becky, wanting to lean forward and touch her lips to the pulse beating heavily at the base of his throat. She cherished every inch of his hard body pressing against hers, his hot, bare chest against hers, his long, muscular thighs against her softer ones. She felt the cool wood on her back, his soft breath caressing her cheeks as he waited, his eyes never leaving hers. Finally they heard the soft clop of a horse outside the window. Gradually it faded.

Eight

Kalli remained still, gazing into Trace's heated eyes as the horse's hoofbeats faded. She could hear the ticking of the clock on the wall. She could feel the racing beat of her heart. Her skin burned where it touched his. Her breath mingled with his as he bent over her, his face only inches from her own, his gaze locked with hers, his dark eyes gleaming.

He, too, waited. She watched as he remained as motionless as a statue, pressed against her, the rapid pulse point at the base of his throat the only sign of life.

Her legs trembled. Heat swirled between her thighs, and her breasts ached for his touch, for his caressing hand, for his hot mouth. She couldn't stand it if he stopped now. She wanted him so much.

"Don't go," she whispered.

"I'm not going anywhere," he said in a low voice. His hand came up to brush a few strands of hair from her face, cupping her cheek, his fingers tracing the curve of her ear. He stared into her liquid eyes, almost drowning in them. He had never felt so alive. Slowly his mouth moved to cover hers. Slowly he brushed his lips against hers, open, damp, warm. She was like honey and sunshine. He kissed her again, feeling her frustration, the desire flaring in her like a hot beacon drawing him nearer, nearer.

Her hands tightened on his back, her fingers brushing against his spine, longing to learn every inch of his body, longing to touch every inch of him.

With a soft groan, Trace pulled back and picked her up. "Our first time is not going to be on the damn floor," he growled, moving to open the door. In seconds, he was striding down the hall to her bedroom.

Kalli's senses spun. Happiness flooded her when he deposited her on her bed and came down right on top of her. Their first time? Did that mean he wanted there to be other times? Lots of times when they'd make love together, sharing each other, learning each other?

His mouth was hot and demanding. His fingers were soft as feathers, yet she felt his touch to her soul. He hurried, which was fine with her, she was burning up for him. The sooner the better, as far as she was concerned. Her hands searched his back, stroking him, learning him. When she met the barrier of his jeans, she tried to slip beneath the waistband, but they were too snug.

His hand captured one rosy nipple, his thumb slowly stroking it, pressing against it. He watched as she responded. Her eyes were glazed with passion, her mouth swollen and damp from his kisses. Her tongue darted out to capture his taste.

Slowly, painfully slowly, he played with her breast, teasing it, tormenting it, until Kalli's fingers were clawing his back, urging him to do more. Deliberately he extended the foreplay. Methodically he brushed against her,

pressed against her while she twisted and moved urgently beneath him.

"Please, Trace, you're killing me," she panted.

His hot mouth moved to draw the tip in. His tongue
brushed against her, savoring her special taste, savoring
the hot feel of her skin. His ears caught her whimper of
pleasure and his body hardened for her. He drove against
her, sucking hard, feeling her buck and writhe as the
tension escalated, stretched taut.

His hand found the fastener on her shorts and slid
down the zipper. She was hot and wet and wanting. The
heat scorched his hand.

Struggling to help him, Kalli shimmied out of her
shorts and panties. She was naked and had hoped the air
would cool her heated flesh. But the flame he built was
too hot, too intense.

"You, too," she said. She wasn't going to do this alone
today. "You, too," she chanted, tugging on the waistband of his snug jeans. Trying to slip the button through
the hole.

"Yeah, me, too." He sat up for a minute and quickly
shucked off his jeans.

Kalli let her passion-glazed eyes sweep over him. He
was beautiful. Strong and muscular, masculine in the
most glorious manner God had designed. She could see
his desire before her, and her heart sped up even more.
The emptiness in her cried out to him. Her body was
quivering with anticipation, demanding a release only he
could give.

Snatching up the jeans, Trace retrieved a foil packet
from the back pocket. Quickly he was ready, leaning over
her, trailing his fingers over her, stroking her feverish
body. Building her craving, raising the tension higher,
ever higher.

"Now, dammit, Trace. Now!"

He knelt between her legs, his hands rubbing slowly, erotically against the soft skin of her inner thighs. Gently he nudged them apart, seeing the glistening welcome awaiting him. Slowly, he pushed into her, covering her with his hard body, catching her face in his hands as his eyes held hers in a gaze that was as hot as the Wyoming sun.

Kalli caught her breath, held it as he filled her. Filled her more than she'd ever been. For a moment she knew she'd found the rest of her. She'd never be alone again. She'd never be incomplete again. She loved him and she was sharing that love with him. She'd give him everything she had.

For a long moment his dark eyes stared into hers. She could scarcely breathe, but she smiled slowly, her heart spilling with love.

"Is this it, cowboy?" she whispered, laughter and longing dancing in her eyes.

"Not by a long shot," he replied, moving against her. He set the pace, and it was fast and wild and hot, just as he'd promised. And Kalli kept up the entire way, her eyes never leaving his, her love reflected for the entire world to see.

When the vortex swirled and caught them, Kalli gave in to it. The splintering satisfaction was white-hot and intense. The shock waves were electrifying, stunning her with the pleasure that coursed through her every cell. The momentum built and built then flashed through her. On and on the stunning waves crashed, burning her, melting her, until she could no longer see Trace, could no longer feel anything but the rapture he brought, the ecstasy of their love consuming her.

Trace held off as long as he could, but the feelings were too intense. He exploded in her, reaching the summit with her, feeling her hot body achieve pleasure when his did. He imprinted her slight frame on his mind as he gave in to the pleasure she brought. Collapsing on her when they were sated, he breathed in the scent of strawberries, and woman, and love. He couldn't move. He knew he was too heavy, he was probably crushing her, but he couldn't move. He'd never felt such satisfaction when making love with any woman. Never felt so at peace. So complete.

Kalli lay still, her hands smoothing across his back, her breathing erratic and harsh, her body humming with the afterglow of perfection. She closed her eyes and held onto the moment. It was perfect. Trace was perfect. And she loved him even more now than before.

Suddenly a shadow dimmed her happiness. What was she going to do? He didn't love her. He didn't even want to try to love her. He wanted her gone.

Slitting open her eyes, she turned her head to see him. Would he change his mind after this? Would he see that together they could build something wonderful? Something lasting? Would he see the possibilities before them, or only remember the painful past and associate her with the woman who had been his wife?

He rolled over, bringing her with him, pressing up into her to show her he was still there. She smiled and lay her head against his chest, savoring every moment she had with him. It had been glorious. The best thing to ever happen to her, beyond even inheriting the ranch.

"You okay?" he asked, his hand sweeping down her soft back, cupping her rounded bottom, pressing her into him.

"Never better." Kalli lifted her head, resting her chin on her stacked hands against his chest and looking at him. Her smile was beautiful.

"Yeah, me, too." His face was still harsh, all angles and planes. But his warm eyes thrilled her. He looked as pleased as she'd ever seen him.

The breeze blew the curtains slightly, passing over their cooling skin. His hand continued tracing random patterns on her back, stopping at her bottom each time to press her closer, closer. Stroking to her shoulders, her neck, tangling languidly in her silky hair.

"Are you getting cold?" he asked.

"Are you kidding? You're like a furnace." She stretched in contentment, rubbing against him like a sated cat. *I love you,* her heart whispered to his, wondering if he could feel it through osmosis. Maybe if she sent thought waves—

He shifted.

"Don't go," she protested.

"I'll be right back," he said, lifting her chin and dropping a quick kiss on her mouth.

She frowned when she heard the shower. He would be gone longer than a few minutes. She debated whether she should join him, but rolled over and curled up instead. She was too tired, too lethargic to move.

He had only been gone a moment, yet Kalli already felt bereft. How could she stand it when he left for the night? When he left for good? She didn't want to think about it. She'd take one day at a time. Maybe she could find the secret to his heart.

When he returned, he drew back the sheets and slid beneath them, drawing her into his arms. With a grateful sigh, she snuggled closer, her arm across his chest, her thigh resting on his.

"I should have showered before."

"Why?" She couldn't keep her eyes open.

"I know I must have smelled of horse and cattle and sweat."

"I don't remember, but now you smell like soap and shampoo."

"Yeah, strawberry shampoo," he said in disgust.

She laughed softly.

"Want to sleep?" he asked.

She nodded, feeling replete, safe, cherished.

Kalli awoke later, after dark, to feel Trace's mouth against her throat, his hands already working to arouse her. Her response was immediate. He was ready. She could feel him hard against her soft belly, his thigh pressed between hers. Smiling sleepily, she turned to him, to embrace him and draw him into her. They made love slowly, gently, deeply. It was as good as the first time, maybe better. It lasted a long, long time.

"Stay the night," she whispered, her mouth loath to leave his. She wanted to fuse to him and never be separated.

"Honey, I can't. My truck's outside, plain as life."

"So?"

"So, you have four men working for you that live a stone's throw away. I don't want to jeopardize your reputation."

"Let me worry about my own reputation. I'm their boss. They're not going to say anything."

"No. I'm not staying." A hint of steel sounded.

"Maybe you're more worried about your own precious reputation," she said sulkily, moving away from him, angry he didn't want to stay when she wanted him to so badly.

"What do you mean by that?" His tone became razor sharp.

"Wouldn't want to jeopardize your lone-wolf reputation, the one where everyone thinks you don't want nor need a woman. Leave then, and show everyone how tough you are."

His hard hand gripped her shoulder, pulling her to face him, pressing her hard into the mattress.

"What the hell does that mean?"

"You're a loner, and you love it. You don't want anyone to think you need a woman. You don't date. You don't do anything as far as I can tell but work on your ranch and covet mine. So I figure even though you're one hundred percent red hot male, you cling to that reputation. And letting it be known you spent the night with a woman would tarnish it beyond repair. We wouldn't want that, now, would we? Gosh, somebody might think it would compromise you."

"What are you pushing for, Kalli? A commitment? Marriage? Hell, I was married. I won't go that route again."

"Well, I haven't been married and maybe I want to be. But not with someone who doesn't like me. All I wanted tonight was for you to sleep over. We've made love twice now. Maybe we could again. But it would be nice after becoming so close, being so *intimate,* just to sleep together."

He stared into her eyes, trying to see her clearly in the darkness, trying to read the emotions that filled her. His eyes revealed nothing.

"Tell me why you don't want to get married again," she said boldly, holding his gaze in the moonlight.

He scowled, pushing away from her, lying back on the bed, his eyes staring blindly at the ceiling. The night air swirled around him, brushing against his chest, cooling his anger. For a long moment he thought back to the end of his marriage, and a different anger built.

"I'm not going to get myself tied up in knots over a woman again." *Like I'm feeling with you.* "Only to have her destroy everything by walking away. It was hell and something I would never deliberately put myself through again."

Kalli propped herself on one elbow and leaned toward him, trying to see his expression in the faint moonlight. "I thought you said you didn't love her," she said softly, soothingly. She longed to hug him, bring him some measure of comfort. But she wanted to hear this. Wanted to understand.

"You don't live with someone for a couple of years, don't have a kid with her, without some feelings. I cared for her, thought we'd build a life together. Then she left, without a word beforehand. Just up and left. Left me. Left Becky. I was twenty-two years old. My grandfather owned the ranch. I had nothing. I didn't know anything but ranching and rodeoing. And then I had a baby to care for alone."

There was bewilderment as well as pain in his voice. Kalli's heart contracted. She ached for the young man he'd been, left alone with a baby. Whatever dreams he had for the future had gone forever when Alyssa walked out.

For a moment she hated the woman. Then reason reasserted itself. If Alyssa hadn't left, Trace wouldn't be free now. And Kalli vowed she would do her best to see he had a happy future. One that included her if at all possible.

"I'm not going to marry you, Kalli," he said quietly.

"No one asked you to," she retorted, trying to ignore the piercing hurt that struck her. Stretching out a hand to rub his chest, longing to throw herself into his arms and hold him all night long, she only said, "Go home, Trace. You've spoiled my mood."

His head turned on the pillow. She could see the gleam of his eyes.

"I really was concerned for your reputation," he said. "Men get brownie points for sleeping with women. It doesn't work the other way around."

"I know."

"Do you want me to stay?"

She hesitated. She ought to tell him to go. She ought to tell him not to come back. She ought to do a lot of things. But she would cling to this one night with all her might.

"Yes, I want you to stay."

"I'll call Betty to let her know I won't be home."

She nodded. Waited patiently as he made the quick call. Then inched across the bed to lie beside him. Relief soaked her when he drew her into his arms and slowly began to stroke her back again. At least she'd have this night with the man she loved.

Trace felt her fall asleep. Her breath fanned across his breast, warm and moist. Her cheek was pillowed against his chest, her trust in him while she slept a wondrous thing. He stared in the night, thinking of the handful of woman in his arms. She was an enchanting thing, but such a contrast. He couldn't figure her out. She was too city to stay, yet her determination seemed endless. Her enthusiasm was naive, yet appealing. He gained a fresh perspective on his life through her eyes. He knew ranching, but until recently he hadn't realized how much he really liked it.

What would it be like to sleep with her every night? To wake up with her and make love in the early morning before he had to see to the cattle and the business of running his spread? To come home to her at night, to her cooking in the kitchen, maybe wearing those short shorts she favored? To take her to bed and love her until they were exhausted?

It was a long time before Trace fell asleep.

When Trace awoke the next morning, he was alone in the big bed. Dressing quickly, he found a new razor in the bathroom and used it. His shirt was on a chair. Kalli must have brought it in from the study. He wondered what he'd find when he located her. Would she be clinging and wanting more than he could give her? Or would she be more reserved around him now? God, he hoped she had no regrets.

He smelled the coffee and headed for the kitchen. She was making pancakes and the fragrance of warmed syrup and coffee filled the kitchen.

"Good morning," she said happily, throwing him a quick smile and turning back to the rising pancakes on the griddle.

"Good morning." He came up to her and tilted her chin to look into her face. Her sunny smile was normal. Her eyes clear and dancing in some kind of amusement. Thank God, he saw no regrets. Trace kissed her. Kissed her again.

"Do you want pancakes or love?" she asked, flicking a quick glance at the stove.

Love? Trace drew back.

"Food. I'm hungry. I didn't get any dinner last night."

"I'd be more concerned if I hadn't seen you scarf down all those brownies before Becky left. How many pancakes can you eat?"

"A dozen." At her startled look, he ran his gaze up and down her body. "How many do you eat, short stuff? One?"

"Shut up or you can fix your own. Short jokes are out."

"Yes, ma'am," he said meekly, his eyes amused.

Now he knew what it would be like to wake up with her. She was as happy as a lark, bubbling over with good humor and anticipation for the day. Breakfast was delicious, though he hardly noticed what he ate, he was too enchanted with her to care about the food.

"You didn't tell me about the hay," she said as she poured herself a second cup of coffee. She had finished eating, but continued to watch Trace put it away. No wonder he was so big, he ate as much as her brother Tony.

Trace paused and looked at her. "What hay?"

"I understand I have a few acres planted in alfalfa hay. It needs to be cut in summer and baled for use in the winter. I can even sell some of it, if I get a good crop."

He nodded.

"So why didn't you tell me about it?"

"Didn't come up."

"You're supposed to be teaching me about ranching. Isn't that a part of it?"

"Kalli, what are you trying to do, make it seem as if I'm deliberately keeping something from you? It isn't time to cut the hay. You've got other things to worry about. Like your roundup. Your finances. Are you current with the IRS? Time enough to get to the hay when it's time to cut the hay."

"Is there anything else you haven't told me?" she asked.

"Hell, yes! There's a lot more you don't know. Let's get the roundup out of the way and we'll tackle the next step. You can't learn everything about a working ranch in one day. I'll teach you what you need to know as we go along."

She nodded, uncertain whether to believe him or not. Had he neglected to tell her because it really wasn't important now? Or was he only doling out the information he felt she had to know? She wasn't ever going to get around the fact he wanted the Triple T. How far would he go to get it?

Trace finished eating, drank the last of his coffee and placed the cup on the table. "Thanks for breakfast. You're a good cook."

She smiled. "Pancakes? Want to try fettuccine?"

He nodded. "Any time."

"How about tonight?" She held her breath.

Trace looked at her, his dark eyes knowing, waiting.

Kalli stood and walked over to him. Before she could sit down, he pulled her across his thighs, cradling her against him.

"Yeah, I'll come again tonight, if you're sure."

Kissing his jaw, she said, "I'm sure."

"Then I'm going home now, get some things done there. What time do you want me back?"

"I don't know, around seven, I guess." The giddy delight bubbled up in her. He would be back for dinner. And the night. She could hardly wait for the day to be gone.

"See you then." He kissed her long and hard, then set her on her feet and rose. Flicking his finger against her chin, he left.

Kalli resolutely headed for the study as soon as the breakfast dishes had been washed. She would finish the blasted computer input today if it killed her. She couldn't wait to have the reports run and get a clear understanding of where she stood. Then she could start to make plans. See what needed to be done to assure the future of the Triple T. For a few minutes she let herself consider what her staying would mean to Trace. When would he believe that she didn't plan to return to Boston? Would his attitude toward her change then? Would he continue to help her on the ranch?

The real question she wondered about was would he continue to see her, make love with her. Or was it a convoluted way to get her to sell? She didn't want to believe that.

Success! Several hours later, with a flourish, she pressed the key to save everything. She was finished! All the bills, receipts, payments from the checkbook had been entered; all the handwritten notes about cows and bulls and sales were in. It was a wonderful feeling. Next month, she'd keep up with everything every day so she only had a few minutes of work to do each time. That was how the hospital ran. How she'd handled her patients' reports, so there wasn't a large amount of paperwork at any one time. And she knew paperwork was not her thing. She preferred people.

"Hello, Kalli." Becky stood in the doorway.

"Hi, honey. Come on in. I didn't hear you come up. Of course I was so busy with this blasted computer, I probably wouldn't have heard your father's truck."

Becky came in, watching Kalli warily. "My dad stayed here last night, didn't he?"

Kalli went still. She couldn't lie to the child. But never once had she thought about making his staying known to Becky. Suddenly she felt awkward, embarrassed.

"He spends too much time here," Becky said without waiting for a reply. "If he didn't have to help you with this ranch, he could be home working on ours."

"He offered to help me," Kalli said uncomfortably.

"You don't know anything about running a cattle ranch. Why don't you go home and let him have it? Then he'd stay home more."

"Once I know enough to manage on my own, he'll be able to stay home more often, as well," Kalli said gently.

Becky flopped down in a chair. "Are all the brownies gone?" she asked nonchalantly.

Kalli smiled in relief. The child wasn't going to pursue why her father hadn't come home last night. "No. I'll get us some. Do you want some milk, too?"

"Sure." Becky shrugged. "You're not on crutches to-day?" she asked as Kalli slowly limped across the room.

"No. My ankle feels lots better. I've kept it strapped, but can manage just fine now without the crutches as long as I walk slowly. I'll be right back."

Kalli wondered how much of Trace's time she was taking from his own work. Too much, if his daughter was to be believed. Was the girl missing her father? She'd come over here a couple of times looking for him. From what she'd said, Kalli suspected they ordinarily spent a lot of time together.

Becky joined her a few minutes later, hesitating in the doorway. "It's stupid for you to carry all that to the office. We can eat here if you like," she said.

"Good idea. Without the crutches, I'm a little shaky on this ankle. The platter of brownies is on the counter. I have the milk."

Soon they were sitting across from each other at the table, Kalli feeling her way in their conversation. Becky seemed nervous, not as comfortable around her as she had yesterday. Had knowing her father stayed the night made a difference? Did she disapprove? Or was she hurt her father hadn't come home?

And how was she going to feel if Trace stayed over tonight?

Casting her mind around for something to say, all Kalli could think about was Trace coming to dinner, staying the night with her again. She felt awkward and unsure around his daughter. Maybe they should take things easier, slower. She was in for the long haul, no need to do everything immediately. And maybe it would show Trace she was here for good. Show him she was interested in a future, not just a fast night in bed.

And if she made a friend of his daughter, maybe he'd be a little more flexible in seeing what good could come of a marriage between them. Kalli knew he felt something for her. She only hoped it was enough to build a future on, that it wasn't only lust. She loved him and wanted to spend her life with him, share their lives.

One stumbling block to that sat before her.

"Would you like to go shopping one day? When my ankle's better?" Kalli asked.

Becky looked up, surprised. "I guess so. But aren't you going to be busy? Dad said you were going to have your spring roundup soon."

"Yes, I'll be busy, though how much of the actual work I'll be able to do, I don't know yet. But it won't take forever, then we can steal away one day and go shopping. Jackson seemed to have a lot of stores."

"Yeah. Most of them cater to the tourists, but some of them are really neat." For a moment the spark of enthusiasm flashed through her expression. Then she dropped her gaze. "I'll have to ask my dad and let you know what he says."

"That's fine. Any time you want."

When Becky left a short time later, Kalli began preparation for dinner. She wanted to take a short nap. She hadn't gotten all that much sleep last night and wanted to be wide awake when Trace arrived. And her ankle was hurting just a little. She knew she should keep off it as much as possible. As soon as everything was ready for dinner, she'd take a quick nap. She had plenty of time before seven.

Nine

Kalli awoke from her nap refreshed. She took a quick shower and donned a deep green sundress. The thin straps revealed the bruise on the back of her left shoulder, but she liked the way it fit and the sexy way she felt wearing it. Trace knew she had the bruise. She didn't wear a bra—the fitted top negated the necessity. Since her ankle was still strapped, she decided to remain barefoot.

Brushing her hair, she let it hang down her back, clipping the sides up in combs. A touch of makeup and she was ready. Scarcely limping, she wandered out to the kitchen. It was almost seven. Checking on everything, she set the big pot of water to boil on the stove and glanced out the window. Trace's truck shimmered in the late afternoon heat. He must have arrived while she was in the shower. Where was he?

"Trace?" She pushed open the screen door and looked in the yard.

"Kalli."

She spun around. He came from the front of the house into the kitchen.

"Hi, when did you get here? I didn't hear you." She smiled and limped over to greet him.

He dropped a light kiss on her lips. He smelled of after-shave, and she drew her fingers against his smooth cheek. Glancing quickly over him, she noted he'd put on fresh clothes, shined his boots. A happy warmth pervaded her. He'd taken care to dress up for her as she had for him. It augured well for the evening.

"I brought you some stockmen's journals, left them on your desk. You can read up on cattle," he said, taking a deep breath. "Something smells good."

"It's dinner. I've had the sauce simmering all day. Sit down and keep me company while I finish. What did you do today?"

"Went into town to do some banking, checked up on a few things. How about you?"

"I finished on the computer! After dinner you can show me how to run the reports, and tell me what they mean." She glanced sassily over her shoulder. "I want to know everything about the ranch, good and bad."

"Mostly it's a good operation. Philip knew what he was doing."

"Mmm. I bet he never expected me to keep the place. It's been years since I visited. Everything was so hectic in Boston, and I always thought I had plenty of time."

"Would it have made a difference to your coming if you'd known about me, about the offer to purchase?" he asked curiously.

"Nope. I did know. Richard wrote me and called. But once I heard the Triple T was mine, I knew I would come out. I love it here. What kind of dressing do you want on your salad?"

"Italian?"

"Not *ranch?*" she flirted.

He chuckled. "Italian."

She set the table, served up their plates and soon sank opposite him. Watching anxiously as he took his first bite, she visually relaxed when he smiled and nodded.

"It's great."

"Thanks. I wanted you to like it."

Dinner was pleasant. During the easy conversation she mentioned Becky's visit and requested his permission to take her shopping.

"To buy what?" he asked, surprised.

"Who knows, maybe nothing. We just want to go shopping."

"Now I know you're crazy, but who am I to stand in your way. Go, by all means. I hate shopping myself."

"Mmm, so I heard. She still wants me to leave, did you know that?"

He looked puzzled. "Why? You just said you'd take her shopping."

"She says I take up too much of your time. She knows you stayed last night."

He frowned. "Hell. I didn't think she'd find out."

Kalli wanted to ask him if that would make a difference in the future. If that would end any thought of something between them tonight. But she kept silent. Let him make his own decisions and tell her what he could do.

"Is your ranch suffering because you're helping me out over here?" she asked.

He smiled and shook his head. "Nope. Everything on the Flying Cloud is running fine. We're ahead of you on branding and repairing our fencing. I've got the time to show you what you need to know."

"Tell me more about the roundup," she invited.

He told her what to expect, how Philip had run things in the past. He told her about various roundups he'd been on at his own ranch and at neighbors' spreads. His stories conveyed all the hard work, yet gave insight into the different men who raised cattle. Their mutual love of the land and the west was evident in all his words.

Their conversation ebbed and flowed as they found different topics to explore together. Trace didn't see many movies, unless shown on TV, but he read extensively and they had a lively discussion on the merits of his adventure books versus her favorite Westerns.

"Ready for dessert?" she asked, rising to clear their plates.

"Depends on what you're serving," he replied, reaching for her as she came close. Pulling her into his lap, he smiled at her, one hand brushing against her flushed cheeks. She looked so pretty.

"Brownies, what else? Even with giving a bunch to the men, we have lots left. Having had ample evidence of your appetite, I'm sure you have room for a few."

"Saying I eat a lot, short stuff?"

"Stop that or I'll sic my brothers on you."

"And are they as short as you?" he asked, his hands molding her dress against her back, tracing the thin straps on her creamy shoulders.

"They're all big. Especially Tony."

"Should I be afraid? Especially sleeping with their baby sister?"

She laughed. "Sleeping? I don't recall getting much sleep last night."

"Well, there was a certain amount of foreplay before sleep."

"Foreplay? That came before making love. Which came before sleeping." Her eyes were sparkling, her smile infectious.

He paused and looked at her, his heart clutching at her teasing words. *Making love.* She was right. They had made love. Hell. The last thing he wanted was to fall for this woman, for any woman. The last thing either of

gled against his hard chest, wanting desperately to stay
awake and savor this quiet time with him. Relish the feel
of his hard body, let her fingers smooth over his tight
skin, feel his blood pump against his pulse points. But she
was exhausted. Her eyes closed and she slept.

The next morning Kalli awoke to a warm kiss. She
slowly opened her eyes and smiled at Trace.

"Nice way to wake up," she murmured, turning to
press her bare chest against his.

"Mmm." It could become addictive, if he'd let it. He
had to back off. He'd made the decision last night, now
he had to carry it out.

"Why don't you shower and I'll fix breakfast," she
said when he made no move to do anything besides hold
her.

"Fine. I have a lot to do today."

As she watched him head to the bathroom she wondered if he was more distant than yesterday. Or was she
imagining it?

Shrugging, she rose and crossed the hall to the second
bathroom, bathing quickly and dressing. Once in the
kitchen, she stacked the dinner dishes and ran hot water
in the sink. Then she drew out eggs and began breakfast.

"Have enough?" she asked as he pushed away his plate
and took a last sip of coffee.

"Plenty, thanks."

"Are you going to show me how to run the reports
now?" she asked brightly. There was something wrong.
She wasn't sure what, but he was definitely more distant. As if this was the first day they met. Their conversation was almost stilted. Was he not a morning person?
Was that all there was to it? No, she'd seen him most
mornings at six, and it was after eight now. He'd never
behaved this way. Something was wrong, but what?

He hesitated, then nodded. "Okay, let's look at what you've got so I can get going. I've things I have to do today."

She nodded and jumped up. Leading the way to the office, she wanted to tell him she wasn't holding him up. Once she knew how to run the reports and analyze them, she wouldn't need help any more. And the plans were well under way for the roundup. If he didn't want to come over for a few days, it was fine with her. She'd manage just fine.

He sat behind the computer and flipped it on. Typing in various commands, he turned on the printer and sat back. Nothing happened.

He pressed a few more keys. Nothing.

Puzzled, Kalli watched over his shoulder.

"What are you doing?"

"Trying to run the reports. Let me try this." He typed a few more commands. Nothing.

He glanced at her oddly, then typed a few more letters.

"Kalli, there's no data."

"What does that mean?"

"I mean, there's nothing here. I thought you put all the information in."

"I did." A sick feeling hit her. "You mean there's *nothing?*"

"Did you save it each day like I showed you?"

"Of course."

"Where's the backup diskette?"

She looked blank. "What is a backup diskette?"

He sighed and looked at the computer. "Something's wrong. You said you finished inputting all the data, but there's nothing here. The last entry is for December."

"Nothing I put in is there?" God, the hours and hours she'd slaved over the blasted machine, and for nothing? Had she done it wrong?

"How can that be? I followed your instructions perfectly. I input into all the cells just as you showed me. I updated each record just like you showed me. I saved it every day, just like you showed me."

"There's nothing here, Kalli. I'm sorry."

She stared at the computer in total disbelief. She couldn't understand how all her hard work had disappeared. She'd followed the instructions perfectly. She knew she had.

Suddenly she glanced at Trace. He was watching her warily. Awaiting an outburst? Or was there more? She couldn't help it. Something was wrong, and not only with her computer. Trace had acted funny all morning. He'd sidestepped their coming here last night by taking her to bed. He had planned to leave first thing, but she'd reminded him of the computer. Now there was nothing there. Horrible suspicions raised their heads.

He had told her how to save the data. What if he'd told her wrong? What if this was just a way to sabotage her efforts so she'd want to give up the ranch? He'd been acting oddly all morning. Had he known there would be nothing here? Had he deliberately taken her to bed last night when she'd mentioned wanting to run the reports to distract her? God, she felt sick. He wouldn't have done that. He couldn't have. There had to be some other explanation.

She cleared her throat. "I guess I have to rekey everything," she said calmly. She would not reveal her thoughts. She wanted to think this through. See if she had made an error. It was possible—she was not used to this kind of computer, nor this program. And she couldn't believe Trace would deliberately mislead her. He was too forthright and demanding. He'd just flat out tell her things she didn't want to hear, not sneak around behind her and erase hours and hours of work.

Yet he was behaving so oddly.

Trace pushed back the chair and stood. She stepped back, feeling overwhelmed by his size, by his closeness. Uneasy with the way her thoughts were heading, she wanted time alone to think.

"Kalli—" he started.

"No, don't tell me again how inept I am about ranching. I'll figure this out and get all the figures put back in." She avoided his eyes. Had he set her up? Had he led her to believe she was doing it correctly, only to have her spin her wheels all this time? She remembered the endless hours she had spent hunched over the damned keyboard. How excited she'd been yesterday when she'd finally punched in the last number and hit the save button.

"Kalli."

"You'd better get on to your ranch. I know you have lots to do." She turned and led the way to the kitchen. Standing stiffly by the table, she avoided his eyes. Trace hesitated only a moment before snatching up his hat. He left without a word. She stood still, fighting tears of frustration as she heard his truck start, depart.

Taking a deep breath, she turned and headed for the office.

Tuesday was the day she'd selected to begin the roundup. Early that morning trucks hauling horse trailers began arriving. Before long her entire yard was filled with dusty pickups, various trailers and over a dozen men and horses.

Kalli hadn't seen Trace in the intervening four days. But she refused to let it bother her. Deep in the night she'd dream of him, dream of them together. But during her waking hours, she was too busy to miss him. Too hurt and proud to call him and ask why he was avoiding her. The suspicions she'd had about sabotage of the computer only solidified with his continued absence. Yet she just couldn't believe he'd ever do something so under-handed.

She greeted her neighbors and their cowhands. Josh was beside her, giving her clues as to who each was and their importance in the area. Many had helped with past roundups, Josh and the other Triple T ranch hands reciprocating. Kalli greeted each in a friendly manner and soon felt at ease with these Western men. She rarely had problems relating to men, due in large part to her brothers and her training in the medical field.

Tom Hyden cornered her with a few friendly words as the men began saddling horses, calling friendly insults to each other and discussing the plan of attack.

"My wife wants you to come to dinner as soon as we have this roundup done. She's dying to meet the proper Bostonian who dared to brave the wilds of Wyoming," he said with teasing grin.

She liked him on the spot. Laughing gently in return, she nodded. "I think I'll disappoint her. Even my folks have to admit they failed to turn me into a *proper* Bostonian. They think they have a maverick in their midst."

"Well, I reckon you'll fit right in here. I see Bob Marshall just pulled in, Trace behind him."

Despite herself, her eyes swung to the drive. She stared hungrily at Trace's truck as it found a spot and settled in. He climbed out at the same time another man got down on the far side. The cowboy went to the trailer ramp and began offloading the horses.

Trace's glance found Kalli and he nodded, his eyes swinging around the yard. He ignored the heat that sparked in his body at the sight of her. Four days had been too damn long. He should have come over sooner and checked on things. Now he forced his mind to the roundup. It should keep him busy enough to keep his mind off Kalli. It was a good turnout. He'd have expected nothing less from his neighbors. They'd all be willing to help, knowing Kalli was new and wanting to show their best side.

He hadn't expected the kick in his gut at seeing her laughing with Tom, however. Hell, Tom was happily married. What was he hanging around Kalli for?

The last few days had been endless. He'd wanted to call her a dozen times. Wanted to come by and see her even more. But he wasn't going to let himself succumb to weak temptation. He was not going to set himself up for a heart load of hurt. She wouldn't last. And he knew it.

Disappointed when Trace continued to ignore her, Kalli still listened carefully as he explained the game plan to the men, pointing out the direction of the camp he'd chosen, assigning rotating tasks. The men were respectful, some of the cowhands even admiring. Surely a man such as he would never stoop to taking advantage of a woman, no matter how much he wanted her ranch.

"Now the camp is close enough so that food can be easily transported from here, but far enough away to keep the flies and cattle and dust from infiltrating the homestead. Any questions before we start?" he finished.

There were one or two, then the men mounted and rode off, each knowing his own responsibility, each ready to do his part.

In only a few moments, Kalli was alone in her yard, with the dust still settling from the many horses. She sighed and turned to the bunkhouse. She and Charlie would be feeding this horde, and he'd said it was a full day's work every day.

By the time they were ready to take dinner to the camp, Kalli had an entirely new appreciation for Charlie and his cooking. There was enough food for a small army. Knowing how much Trace ate, she could imagine each of the men would put away just as much. Her brothers always ate enough individually to supply a family of four.

Charlie handled the logistics of moving the food and keeping it hot easily from years of practice. Ready to go, they climbed into the truck and headed for the action.

It seemed like utter chaos when Kalli and Charlie first crested the rise that separated the branding area from the home base, but in only seconds she could see some sort of rough choreography. Each man performed his assigned task. There were the ropers who lassoed the calves and drew them to the men on the ground. The teams on the ground flipped the calves to their sides, quickly castrated, then notched one ear while a third man pressed the hot brand onto the flank. In less than two minutes, the calf was released to run bawling back to the herd, seeking its mother.

More men drove cattle from the far reaches of the ranch. Several kept the branded calves from mingling with the unbranded.

It was hot, dusty and noisy. Kalli watched in stunned awareness for a long moment, long after Charlie climbed out of the truck and began setting up the chow. It was awesome. And not the romantic notion she had of cattle drives. The noise was appalling, calves bawling, men swearing, searing sizzles of the brands, deep bellows of the mother cows. Horses snorted and hooves pounded. The stench of burning flesh, blood and sweat mingled with the dust flying in the field that had earlier in the day boasted green grass. The sun beat relentlessly on the scene. Wrinkling her nose in distaste, Kalli thought back to her pristine hospitals. The sterile atmosphere was sometimes sundered by the trauma of the injured, but quickly restored. What a contrast.

"You helping, or just sitting?" Charlie asked as he paused in one trip from the truck's cab to the trestle set up for the men.

"Helping." She scrambled from the truck and threw herself into the work. Still, she absorbed everything.

Searching, she found Trace. He looked hot and tired. Even from this distance, and over the other noise, she heard him swear when a calf kicked his thigh. Was she attuned to his voice?

When Charlie banged the metal trash can top as an announcement the meal was ready, several men came over to the trestle and served heaping plates. The rest continued to work. When the first group was done, they replaced others. The process was repeated until everyone had eaten.

Kalli talked, laughed and asked a million questions. Everyone was willing to tell her all she wanted to know and then some. She enjoyed meeting her neighbors, enjoyed their banter and jokes. The only dark spot was the way Trace avoided her. But she tossed her head and smiled at everyone else. No one would guess her heart felt bruised and battered.

Three days. Trace watched the last of the calves move slowly toward the camp. They'd finish today if he had to keep them at work until midnight. He couldn't keep seeing her every day and not speak to her, touch her. These had been the longest three days of his life. He saw Kalli every time she came near. She was always cheerful and friendly. Hell, half the cowboys working had a crush on her already. She knew just what to say, just how to be friendly without crossing any lines that would lead to further expectations. Bob and Tom thought she was great. The food she'd ordered and served couldn't compare with anything Philip had served over the years, tasty and plentiful.

And she ignored him as if he had been invisible.

Which is what he wanted, he told himself. He knew they had no future, but dammit, it hurt. He wanted her to talk to him, flirt with him. Miss him.

He didn't like the way she flirted with the other men. Of course, others might not see it as such, but just looking at a man with those bright dark eyes of hers, just grinning at someone as if she was sharing a private joke that only the two of them knew—hell, things like that could get a man thinking thoughts he had no business thinking.

Trace knew he ought to ride right up to where she was now and let Rory Jefferies know that Kalli would be leaving soon. Make sure Bob and Tom warned their single cowboys about falling for a city girl who was here as part of a fantasy and would be leaving at the first sign of trouble.

But he kept away, afraid he'd lose what little control over his temper he had and punch one or another of the men right in the face.

He frowned, urging his horse toward the small band of cows and calves coming down the hill. He'd worked as hard as anyone these last few days. Tried to exhaust himself so he'd sleep at night. But he only remembered Kalli sleeping with him. How soft and sweet and feminine she was tucked up against him in that bed of hers. How fragrant she smelled, like a woman, not like a stinking cow or a bleeding calf. Her voice was full of laughter and excitement. Not grumbling and swearing like cowboys.

Hell, he didn't want anyone looking at her but him. And there wasn't a damned thing he could do about it. He kicked his horse and tried to outrun his thoughts.

Ten

Kalli struggled with the heavy saddle. She'd rigged up a cross hitch near the corral, set a sturdy wooden box beside it. Using that, she gained enough height to heave the saddle across the horse's back. Now to cinch it up. It wasn't easy, but she wanted to see some of the roundup from horseback. And they said today would be the last day. Her ankle was better. Even standing on it for long stretches while serving meals these last couple of days hadn't caused a problem. Time to see a bit of the action from the back of a horse.

She yanked up on the cinch for all she was worth, then flipped down the stirrups and reached around for the reins. She unhooked the cross hitch. Still on the box, she stepped into the saddle and settled herself. She'd done it. Just another example of how Yankee ingenuity paid off. She didn't need anyone saddling her horse for her anymore.

"So, want to show me what a good cow pony you are?" she asked as she kicked the gelding lightly with her heels. He began walking toward the open fields. She urged him into a faster gait until they were loping toward the camp. In only a couple of minutes the thundering roar of horses sounded as she crested the hill above the branding site. She spotted Trace, Josh and José riding hell-for-leather straight after a fleeing group of calves. Smiling, she drew up and watched as they turned them, slowed them and headed the recalcitrant group to the camp.

Urging her mount forward, she intercepted Trace as he drew near the branding site.

He drew up and watched her ride to him.

"Hi," she said brightly, ignoring the fact he hadn't spoken to her in a week.

"What are you doing here?"

"I came to take part in the roundup. I'm tired of cooking. I want some of the action."

"You don't belong here. You don't have the first idea of what to do. It's dangerous, Kalli, not some picnic."

"I believe it's still my ranch. And my place to participate in my roundup. You're in charge, what should I do?" Jutting her chin out, she glared at him. She would not be sent home like a child!

"Tim!" Trace roared, calling the young man as he cut out a bawling calf. "Ride with Kalli, show her the ropes." Trace touched the brim of his hat and rode away without a backward look.

Turning her horse toward Tim, Kalli tried not to let the hurt take hold. But it was impossible. After a week of not speaking, he'd treated her like a disliked acquaintance. Damn the man!

"Hi, Kalli. I was just getting ready to bring in another bunch. Come on and I'll show you how." At least someone was glad to see her, she thought as she partnered with Tim.

"Cows are dumber than dirt," Kalli mumbled as she shampooed her hair a second time, letting the hot water course over her aching body. "Almost as dumb as a certain rancher I know," she said, getting the last of the dirt and grit from her long hair. Chasing calves and separating them from their mothers had proved much more difficult and dirty than she would ever have suspected. Dust almost an inch thick had covered her. Her ankle ached again from staying in the saddle as the cutting horse had darted and turned, doing his job. Her arms were weak from swinging ropes. And she had lasted only four hours. Those men did it day in and day out, all day long. No wonder Trace's muscles were so well-defined.

Paired with Tim, she had little time to seek Trace out. But she caught glimpses of him during the afternoon, and found his eyes on her from time to time. Refusing to let him know how his reactions were confusing her, she smiled each time, pleased to note his frown when he realized she'd seen him before he returned to whatever task he was doing. At least he wasn't indifferent to her.

"Dumb bastard," she said as she shut off the water and snatched a thick towel to dry with. What game was he playing? If he thought he was going to chase her away to get her ranch or get her to leave, he was dead wrong. She didn't think he was thinking at all. Just reacting. What had caused his distant attitude? What had changed, that last night? She had thought it spectacular. Had she said something to offend him?

As long as she lived she would never understand the male of the species, she thought as she drew on a loose caftan. She turned on the hair dryer and began to dry her hair, puzzling on the mystery of Trace Longford.

His warm hand covered hers and flicked off the dryer. Startled, Kalli spun around.

"You scared me to death!" she said. But the fear vanished instantly when she saw him. He was covered in the dust and mud and blood from the branding. His face was worried.

"We've got a man injured. Can you look at him? We might need to call an ambulance."

"Of course. Where is he?" She followed Trace to the kitchen where she saw a young man propped up in one of her chairs. Blood was coursing down his face. His shirt was torn and bloody. Tim and Bob Marshall supported him as he sagged against them.

"What happened?" Kalli asked as she hurried to the injured man.

"Ran into an irate mama cow," he said, trying to make light of the serious situation.

"Looks like she won. Can you men put him up on the table? It'll do for an exam. Tim, run to the bunkhouse and get that first-aid kit we got a couple of weeks ago. Bob, help me get his shirt off. Trace, can you run the water until it's hot, but not so hot it burns?" Calmly Kalli directed the men on the various tasks she wanted done as she assisted the cowboy onto her dining table. Kalli's training and work as an emergency nurse stood her in good stead. She worked swiftly and efficiently. Grateful she'd had the foresight to get Charlie to purchase a large industrial first-aid kit on his last visit into town, she knew she had enough supplies for emergency first aid. Now to see the extent of the injuries.

As she worked and joked with Jerry Williams, the injured man, she was conscious of Trace's eyes on her. He leaned against the wall and watched her work, watched as she joked and washed away the blood. Watched as she assessed the extent of damages and made a call to the local hospital. Watched as she bandaged the injured man and helped Bob and Tim get him to her spare room.

"Get a night's sleep and then we'll see how you feel. If everything's fine in the morning, you're free to go. The cut didn't even need stitches, and if you don't show signs of a concussion, I declare the altercation a draw," she said as she eased a light blanket over him.

"Sorry to be so much trouble," he mumbled, giving in to the pain pills she'd given him.

"Not a bit of trouble. I've missed nursing, didn't realize how much until right now. I'll check on you during the night. If you wake and need something, call me. I'll leave the door open."

Kalli thanked Bob and Tim and followed them to the kitchen. Trace had gone. Bidding them good night, she set about cleaning up the mess. When her kitchen was set right, she wandered out to the front porch and sat down. Most of the trailers were gone now. The roundup had ended, the calves were branded, and the herd was turned loose to graze until fall.

Kalli watched as the stars came out, piercing the dark blanket that hid the mountains from view, that blotted out everything in its vast expanse. Slowly she began to think. It was time to let go. She couldn't have everything she wanted. And wanting alone didn't make it possible. She'd given it her best, but some things were just not meant to be.

In the morning she'd deal with it. But for right now she wanted to sit on her porch and think and remember. Tears blurred her vision as she blinked frantically to clear her eyes. She loved him so much, ached with the knowledge he didn't want her. She wanted to stay with him, build a future together. But he only wanted her land. Slowly she rose and went to bed.

* * *

Kalli checked on Jerry several times during the night, but he slept through. Upon waking in the morning, he insisted on getting up and going home. "Though I appreciate all you did for me, ma'am," he said as he finished the last of the eggs she prepared him.

"It was the least I could do, you did so much for me with the roundup. I'm only sorry you were injured helping out. As soon as I'm dressed, I'll give you a ride home."

"The boss said he'd send someone," Jerry protested.

"No problem, I have to go into town for some things anyway. I'll be ready in a few minutes."

The next three days Kalli spent hours on horseback, seeing every inch of the ranch. Each night she'd soak in the tub, trying to keep her muscles in some sort of working order.

She heard nothing from Trace.

The spring roundup was over, the new tally of cattle official. She baked about a million cookies and took them as a thank-you to each of the ranches that had helped. She met Mary Margaret Hyden and agreed to go to dinner one night. She met Bob Marshall's wife and four children and agreed to meet them at church on Sunday.

She arranged to sell her hay when she harvested it.

Still she heard nothing from Trace.

Kalli called her parents and discussed things with them for a long time. Feeling slightly homesick, she was glad for the opportunity to talk to them, get their input on what she was doing. Two of her brothers called and she regaled them with all the benefits of ranch life, only admitting at the end that she missed them terribly and wanted to see them again, soon.

Evenings Kalli sat on her porch. Watching the sun set behind the Tetons, she gathered her feelings close and rejoiced in her ranch. She loved Wyoming. She felt its peace and wonder pervade, wash through her like a blessing. She thought long and hard about her future, about ranching and about Trace. Mostly she thought about Trace.

Finally her mind was made up. On Wednesday morning she drove to town, to see Richard Strominger.

It was afternoon by the time Kalli returned to the Triple T. She'd thought it through for days and made her decision. Now the plan was in motion. Before long, she was sure, she'd hear from Trace Longford. She only wondered what she'd hear.

Two days later Kalli was in the kitchen when the knock at the door caught her unawares. She'd been so caught up in her thoughts, she hadn't heard anyone arrive.

Becky stood in the doorway when Kalli opened it, her face pale.

"Can I talk with you, Kalli?" she asked, looking bewildered.

"Oh, honey, anytime. Come on in."

Suddenly Becky burst into tears. Kalli reached out and drew the child to her, enfolding her in her arms. Becky was as tall as Kalli, but she didn't let that bother her. She rocked her as they stood in the doorway, smoothing her hair, gently crooning to her, wondering all the while what had happened to make the child so upset.

"It's my fault," Becky sniffed after a moment, obviously trying to get herself under control.

"What is, honey? What's got you so upset?"

Becky just sobbed.

As a nurse, Kalli had experience soothing distraught relatives. She knew what to say, how to say it, and gradually Becky's weeping stopped. With her arm around Becky's shoulders, Kalli led her to the table and pressed her down into a chair.

"I'll get you a washcloth and you'll feel better."

Kalli bathed her face, then went to the sink and ran the cloth under cold water. She wrung it out and handed it to Becky.

"The cool water will keep your eyes from swelling."

Becky's eyes filled again.

"Now tell me what's the matter." Kalli brushed back her hair, gripped her shoulder, trying to offer comfort to the girl.

"I wanted you to go away." Becky said tearfully.

Kalli sat down, watching the child.

"I know that. You and your dad wanted me to leave."

"I wanted you to go away so Dad would stay home and spend the summer with me like we did other years. And he wanted this ranch. I thought if you left, he'd get it."

"But this is my home," Kalli said gently.

"Dad said you'd never stay. At the first setback, you'd be gone. Since you wouldn't stay, I thought you should go now, not stay through the summer. I only wanted you to leave."

"And so you're upset because I'm still here?" Kalli asked gently.

"No. It's not working, and Daddy's worse than he's ever been. He's so grouchy all the time."

Since when, Kalli wondered, her heart skipping a beat. Since their last night together? Was he missing her as much as she missed him?

"I tried to get you to leave, and you just don't go," Becky said, a hint of bewilderment in her gaze. "I tried with the horse, I thought you'd leave then. But you didn't. Then I fixed your computer, and you still didn't leave."

"Hold on a second. What are you saying? Did you do something to Stony so he'd buck?"

Becky nodded, tears coursing down her cheeks.

"And you erased all my computer work?"

She nodded again. "Daddy said if things went wrong, you'd leave."

"Your dad is dead wrong. I'm staying. He just has a problem understanding that. But I thought you and I were starting to be friends. I thought we'd go shopping together and do some more baking—"

Becky started crying again. "I liked you, Kalli. But I wanted to make my dad happy. And I thought getting this ranch would make him happy." She lay her head on her hands and cried.

Kalli was more confused than ever. She ached for the girl's unhappiness, rejoiced that Trace had not been the one to sabotage her computer efforts, but didn't know how to handle Becky's revelations. The child had only been trying to help her father. Being without a mother, their relationship was closer than others, and Becky fought for her father just as he would have fought for her. Kalli grew a little indignant that Trace's constant harping on her unsuitability had taken root in such a convoluted manner. But it was time for all such shenanigans to stop.

"You'll have to tell your father, Becky. And you have to stop doing things like that."

Becky looked forlorn. "He'll be mad at me."

"Damn straight, he'll be mad. I'm a bit miffed myself," Kalli said, rising. "What you did was wrong, don't you know that?"

Becky nodded. "But I didn't mean for anyone to get hurt. I'm sorry about your ankle. I've fallen lots of times and never got hurt."

"How'd you do it? I thought Stony was just skittish."

"A thistle beneath the saddle blanket." Becky shrugged. "I didn't think you would suspect. You being a city lady and all. And then I took off the blanket and threw the thistle away."

"Well, for future reference, older women aren't as agile as young girls. And that horse is a lot taller than yours. I could have been seriously injured."

"I know. I was so scared when you fell and didn't get up right away."

Kalli remembered Becky had asked if she was dead. Shaking her head, Kalli took Becky's arm and helped her up, then gave her a handful of tissue. This was Trace's problem, not hers. Marching Becky to the bathroom, Kalli instructed her to wash her face and comb her hair.

"When you're done, come out on the front porch. We'll have some lemonade and talk a bit more. Then you'll have to go home and tell your dad."

Kalli fixed lemonade and got some cookies. She took them out to the porch and sat down, her thoughts churning. She had never suspected Becky. For a guilty moment she remembered suspecting Trace, even knowing he wouldn't do such a thing.

Becky came out and sat gingerly on the edge of a chair, looking lost and uncertain.

Kalli handed her a glass and offered her the plate of cookies. "How'd you sabotage the computer?"

"When you went to get brownies that afternoon, I just did a global erase."

Kalli frowned. "How did you know to do that? I know nothing about computers beyond inputting on predesigned screens."

"Dad taught me a lot. I've had some in school. I know a lot about them. And the program you use is so easy."

"Great. I hired a high school kid to rekey all the information you erased. If I'd known about you, you could have done it."

"Daddy will probably pay you back," Becky said sadly. "He's going to be so mad at me."

"Yeah, probably. But he loves you and will understand you were only trying to help him."

Becky sniffed but said nothing.

Kalli wished she could talk to her mother, ask her opinion on how to handle Becky. And maybe even how to handle Becky's obstinate father. She loved him, but he pushed her away at every turn. He'd ignored her for over a week. Insisted he knew she wouldn't stay. What would it take, ten years in residence before he'd allow that maybe she'd stay a little while?

What was she going to do about Becky? Rather, what would Trace do? He was the child's father. For a moment Kalli was glad she had no children. She wanted them, and would love them to death when she had them, but they could be a trial. Briefly she smiled, remembering the headaches she and her brothers had given their parents. Such was family life. There was a lot of joy shared, as well.

"He'll probably yell at me," Becky said in a sad voice.

"Yes, but yelling can only hurt your eardrums," Kalli said easily. "And I'll protect you if he gets too bad."

Becky looked at her in amazement. "You're not even as big as I am."

"Ah, but I'm a lot tougher, sweetheart. Comes from standing up to five brothers. All of which are about the size of your father."

Trace stared at the letter from Richard Strominger, unable to believe what he was reading. He felt sick. He couldn't believe what he'd read. Kalli was offering to lease him her ranch. *She was leaving.* After all her protestations of staying for the long haul, she was leaving.

He should be feeling good. He'd wanted the ranch, could expand his herd, start that new breeding program. He'd known all along that she'd leave. He'd drawn back from her warmth and happiness to save himself the pain of her leaving. But he felt as if he'd been gutted. He felt betrayed and abandoned.

Damn, he thought, leaning back and closing his eyes to dispel her image dancing before him. It didn't work. He could see her as clearly as he had that first day, climbing so sassily from her new truck. See her as clearly as he had in her bed that morning when she'd come apart in his arms. See her as clearly as he had riding when she was so sore she could scarcely sit on the saddle.

His gut tightened and he opened his eyes. Clenching his jaw tightly, he tried to ignore the pain that cut like a knife, tried to remind himself he'd known all along she'd leave. But being right this time didn't ease the ache that plagued him. Somehow he'd hoped he would be wrong.

I'm in for the long haul, she'd said. Yet he'd known she wouldn't stay. Alyssa hadn't. Kalli was from Boston, light-years away from a lonely, isolated ranch in Wyoming. He'd known it, but it didn't make the reality any easier.

Hell, he didn't want her damn ranch any more. Not if it meant losing her. He wanted her. He wanted her to stay with him, live with him, be there for him. To share her life with his until they were both old. Until one of them died. He wanted her to give him more children. He'd always liked children, loved Becky. He'd love to have children with Kalli. They'd probably be as feisty and troublesome as their small mother. Was it true all her brothers were large? He would want their sons to be tall, but all the daughters could be pocket size, like Kalli.

He wanted her in his bed every night. He wanted to make love to her until neither one of them could breathe. Sleep with her, feel her warm, soft, silky body snuggled against his every night, especially in the long, dark nights of winter. He wanted to wake her up each morning with kisses and love and see her sparkling eyes laughing at him.

He didn't care a snap of the fingers about the Triple T, he wanted its owner. Only now it was too late. She had stopped fighting him, relinquished her ranch to him. To make him happy, the damn letter said. Hell, if she left, nothing would ever make him happy again.

Eleven

Kalli heard the throaty growl of Trace's big pickup before she saw it. She looked down the gravel drive and watched as he drew nearer. For the first time in days she felt alive, gloriously alive. He was coming, and they would certainly have a few words to say. She smiled in anticipation. Her visit to Richard had been a gamble. But just maybe it was one she'd win.

She couldn't see him clearly behind the tinted glass, but she knew he was angry as hell from the way the truck roared toward her house. It stopped with a swirl of dust and gravel. She smiled. It was time this know-it-all rancher found out something new.

"Becky, do me a favor and take some of these cookies down to Charlie at the bunkhouse," Kalli murmured, her eyes never leaving the truck. This was do-or-die time. Oddly, she was almost calm.

Becky hurried away without an argument, glad to delay confessing to her father what she'd done.

Kalli tipped back in her chair and watched, her heart pounding. Trace had obviously received Richard's letter. Now she waited to see his reaction. She wouldn't give in to the uncertainty that plagued her. She would see what he had to say.

Trace slammed the truck to a stop and cut the engine. Anger and fear raged. He wasn't sure which was stronger. He only knew since meeting Kalli Bonotelli he'd had more emotions flare than any time in his life. Now that he was here he hesitated, fear roiling in his gut. He was going to confront her about the letter. Challenge her about all the fine talk she'd given over the weeks and see what she said. And he was afraid she'd tell him goodbye.

He snatched up the letter from the seat and thrust open the truck door, slamming it closed behind him like a shot. He crossed the short distance smoothly, deadly, like a lone wolf on the prowl. Kalli shivered in delight, holding his gaze with her own, watching as he slowly walked toward the porch, his eyes caught with hers, his gaze hard and impassive.

Damn, but she looked cool, tipped back in the chair, watching him with a speculative look on that pretty face. He'd like to shake her up, shake her, period, for putting him through everything. Damn her, why had she come to Wyoming at all if she wasn't going to stay?

There were two shallow steps up to the wide wooden porch. Trace rested his foot on the first step. Shimmering waves of anger filled the air. Kalli slowly brought her chair down and stood, wiping her palms against her shorts.

"Hi, Trace," she said, watching him warily.

He was surprised to see a glimmer of fear in her expression. Of him?

"What the bloody hell do you think you're doing?" he asked menacingly, waving the crumpled letter in front of her nose.

She glanced at it then at him. "I assume that must be the letter from Richard. Wasn't he clear?"

He was tall, threatening and so heart-stoppingly male she felt the feminine parts of her soften in desire. She licked her lips and studied him with false calmness. At least there was a reaction. Not a quiet acceptance. Somehow the gamble had to pay off.

"You're leasing me the ranch."

She shrugged. "You said you wanted it. You've been saying it since I arrived."

"I wanted to buy it, dammit, not lease it. I wanted you to sell it and get the hell back to Boston so I wouldn't have to see you again! Leasing it would tangle us up together forever."

"I told you I wasn't selling," she said primly, still trying to gauge his reaction. Was it only anger?

"Hell, you also told me you weren't leaving, but what are you doing but heading back to the east coast as fast as you can? And being ornery about relinquishing the ranch."

"I'm—"

"Can't take it, just as I said, can you?" he snarled, stepping up on the first step. "What about all your protestations about staying in Wyoming for the long haul? What was all that malarkey about your being one determined woman?"

She cocked her head to one side, narrowing her eyes in a wary look. "What about it?" she asked. "Maybe there comes a time when you have to cut your losses. Realize things won't ever be the way you want, no matter how much you want them. Admit it and move on."

He closed his eyes, rubbed the fingers of one hand against his closed lids, then snapped them open.

"Don't go, Kalli," he said softly, urgently.

"Why not?" She held her breath.

"Because I want you to stay."

Her heart sped up. Her skin tightened and flushed. Hope blossomed. "Why?"

He hesitated, his eyes gazing deeply into hers. He swallowed hard. "Because I want you, dammit!"

"That's all?" Disappointment threatened.

"Isn't that enough?" He put his boot on the next step.

She shook her head. "That sounds like only sex."

"It's not only sex. I want you in bed, I can't deny that. But I want you out of it, too."

Her heart thumped harder and harder. *Come on,* she urged, *say it, oh, please, just say it.* She took a step closer and smiled at him.

"So I should stay just because you want me?"

He nodded, licking suddenly dry lips.

She shook her head. "It's not enough."

"Hell, what do you want? I've never asked anyone else to hang around. We have something special between us. Stay and see what happens." Fear rose again. She was going to leave, and all because he couldn't say what he felt. Couldn't voice the emotions that threatened to swamp him. Fear spread through him like a plague. Dammit, he was going to lose her just because he was a coward.

"I need more than wanting."

"I need you to stay."

"Here? Run my ranch with your help?" She tried for clarity. If he wanted her that much, how much bigger was the step from that to love? She wanted it all. She was greedy and demanding, and he would say the words to her before she'd say yes.

"I thought you wanted the Triple T," she said, stalling for time. Trying to figure out a way to get him to admit he loved her. He had to, didn't he, to ask her to stay? *Please, God, let him love me.*

"When I heard from Richard that you were leaving, I knew the ranch didn't mean anything to me. I want you."

"Richard told you I was leaving?" She frowned. Had he really said that?

"The letter said you were leasing me the land. Hell, lady, you can't leave."

"Why not?" Her fingers slipped between the buttons on his shirt, rubbed lightly against his warm skin. She breathed in the tangy scent of him, the mixture of horses and sunshine and masculine strength.

"Why not?" He rested his forehead against hers, his breath fanning across her cheeks. "Kalli, you're the sunshine in a dark life. You are laughter and enthusiasm and delight. You've brought me more than I can ever give you. I can't let you go."

"You're always giving orders."

"Yeah, and you're always arguing with me. Only don't argue with me on this one, Kalli. Stay."

"Give me a good reason, cowboy, and I'll see what I can do." Kalli smiled, love spilling out of her heart for this man.

He read the demand in her eyes. "You've never done anything to make it easy for me."

She grinned and shook her head slowly, but took a step closer. They were almost touching from chest to thigh. "You're tough, Trace, you don't need anything made easy."

"Stay with me, Kalli. Live with me. Build a life with me. Don't go back to Boston." He was getting desperate. She was toying with him, damn her, and he wasn't sure he was getting through to her.

Her face was on a level with his, her body so close now he could feel the heat radiating from her. Could feel her breath stir the air near him. Could smell the sweet scent of her hair, the fragrance of wildflowers from her warm body. He took a deep breath, knowing he would always recognize her in a dark room by her sweet scent alone.

"Tell me why you want me," she breathed, one finger trailing down his cheek, feeling the muscle tighten in his jaw when he clenched his teeth. "Is it so very hard?"

"Damn you, yes!" He swept her up in his arms and lowered his mouth to hers, ruthlessly plunging into the heat of her. His lips found a hot response, his tongue its mate. His hands molded her against him, running up and down her spine, cupping her bottom and hauling her closer still. He relished the feel of her full breasts pressing against his chest, the softness of her belly against his. If he lived to be a hundred and had her every day he'd never get enough of her. She was his life, his happiness, his future. He had to have her, now, tomorrow, forever.

Setting her on her feet, he rested his forehead against hers. His breath was harsh and rapid. "I'm incomplete without you," he growled.

She pressed her lips against his gently, speaking as they clung. "Incomplete?"

Incomplete described her life perfectly when Trace was not there. He'd completed her in a way she would never have known if she had not come to Wyoming.

"Yeah."

"There's more. Say it, Trace. Say it!"

His eyes opened to find hers, gaze deep into hers as he said slowly, "Hell, you make me so mad I want to strangle you. But I won't...because I love you, Kalli. As hard and deep as any man can. I don't want to. I was content with my life before you came and I know you're going to bring me a truckload of heartache, but I can't help it. I love you beyond belief. Stay!"

Snuggling closer, she brushed her lips across his again. "I'm not bringing you anything but love, Trace. I've loved you for weeks. Maybe since the first time I saw you.''

He hugged her tightly, his mouth tender as he nibbled kisses across her cheeks, on her nose, her eyelids, avoiding her lips as he teased her into arousal. His tongue flicked against her soft skin, his breath bathed her face. The feelings of relief and love swelled in him until he couldn't tell what was what. She loved him! God, she was going to stay and love him.

''Kiss me,'' she demanded, almost frantic with love and desire.

He complied, and the embrace was endless, gloriously endless.

''Becky said you haven't been happy lately,'' she murmured, when he pulled back to breathe. Her heart melted at his love words. Who would have thought her cowboy capable of such a romantic turn?

''When I'm with you I am.'' God, he loved her so much. Was she really going to stay? ''These last days have been hell. And then to get this blasted letter from Richard—''

''Tell me what Richard said,'' she murmured, snuggling against him, wanting to rip the shirt from his chest and press her bare breasts against him. Wanting to draw his mouth to hers and plunder it. To capture the spiraling ecstasy only he brought. To reaffirm together the love they'd just confessed.

''Who the hell cares what Richard said?'' He was frustrated. She wasn't saying yes. Though she hadn't said no, either.

''Tell me.''

He flung himself away and walked across the porch, leaning his forearm against a post. He gazed out across the grassy acreage that he'd longed to own.

''You're driving me nuts, you know that?'' he asked.

''You'll get used to it. Tell me.''

"He said you were willing to lease the Triple T to me. And split the cattle proceeds if I'd take them on. The ranch was not for sale."

"That's right."

He turned back. "Why?"

"I told you."

"Were you going to say goodbye, or were you going to just leave without a word?"

"Did Richard tell you there were a couple of restrictions to the deal?" she asked.

"Yeah, he mentioned something about that. But I didn't call to find out the details, I had to see you." Had to make sure she was still here. Had to convince her to stay. Even now he had doubts.

"I wanted you to keep Charlie and Tim and Josh and José on. This is their home, and I didn't want them done out of it."

"No problem, they're good men. And I would have needed more cowhands with the increased land. But I've changed my mind. I don't want the land, now, I want you. I had to face it when I got the letter. When I thought of all it meant. I've done a good job with Flying Cloud, but my life has been very one-sided for years. Except for Becky, I do nothing that doesn't pertain to the ranch. Your coming changed that. I don't want to change back."

"I get unlimited access to the property, whenever and wherever I want," she continued as if he hadn't spoken.

He frowned at her. "What do you mean?"

"And I get the house, barn and ten acres surrounding it. Your men can live in the bunkhouse same as always, if you like."

He stared at her.

"I'm not leaving," she said softly, watching him as he realized what she had done. "I was never leaving. I told you I was here for the duration."

"But you gave up your ranch?"

"I told you, I've thought about it a lot. I love it here, but you were right, I'm not a rancher. I don't know enough and don't think I can learn. I'm not crazy about cattle, the roundup showed me that. I'm certainly not crazy about that damn computer. I loved visiting Uncle Philip, thought I could settle in and run it, but it's more than I can handle. Plus, I like people. I'd rather help people who need me than worry about roundups or cutting hay or doing taxes. I told you, it's time I admit it's not for me and move on. I've applied for a nurse's job at the hospital in Jackson. I'm not cut out to be a rancher."

Trace stared at her, stunned. *She wasn't leaving.* Even if he hadn't rushed over here today she would have stayed. Slowly the last vestiges of fear faded. Slowly he let himself hear what she'd said, all she'd said.

"How about a rancher's wife?" Trace asked. Time stood still as he waited for her answer.

"Maybe, for the right reason," she said, that slow smile lighting up her face.

"And that is?" He wanted her so badly he could taste it. He took a step closer, trying to read her expression, trying to figure out what reason she could demand, so he could make everything come right.

"Love," she said gently, her eyes sparkling at him, shining with love for him.

"God, Kalli, I love you more than life itself," he said, reaching for her, lifting her in his arms, spinning her around. "You already have that. Marry me, live here with me, love me. Forever."

She laughed in delight, hugging him close, her feet still off the ground. "Yes, yes, *yes!* I love you, Trace. I'd be so proud to be a rancher's wife. Your wife."

Her mouth found his and Kalli knew she was home. The gamble, to offer him her ranch with no strings, had paid off, and she had won. She was home, forever.

Epilogue

Kalli stood by the window, the soft smile reflecting her happiness. She could hear the guests in the yard. Her brothers' voices were loud and boisterous, as they always had been. It had been a wonderful week, having her entire family visit.

Her mother settled Kalli's gown one more time. Fluffing the veil, she regarded her daughter with tears in her eyes.

Kalli turned and reached out to hug her mother. "It'll be fine, Mom. I'm so happy, be happy for me."

"I am darling. But Wyoming is so far from home and you'll be here all alone with him."

"Trace is more than enough to fill my days." And nights, but best not to have her mother thinking about that. "And I have a new daughter to spend time with."

"Trace is a fine man. A bit quiet, but he seems to dote on you."

Kalli grinned and nodded. It worked both ways, she doted on him.

A soft knock sounded at the door.

Kalli's mother answered and smiled at the young girl dressed up before her.

"Hi, Becky, want a minute with Kalli?" Sensing their need for privacy, Mrs. Bonotelli turned to the door. "I'll go out and be seated. They can't start without the mother of the bride. Your dad will be along any minute."

"Okay, Mom, see you out front."

The entire Bonotelli clan had gathered for her wedding to Trace. In addition, half the neighboring ranches had come, as well as all the ranch hands from both ranches. The August day was perfect. There was not a cloud in the sky. The wedding was to be held at noon, allowing time for the bride and groom to enjoy the reception before departing on their honeymoon. She was going to see Yellowstone at last.

"Becky?" Kalli moved over to the girl. "What is it, honey? Is everything okay?"

Becky fiddled with the sash on her dress. She was to be Kalli's maid of honor and the pale yellow dress she'd chosen to wear was perfect. "I guess. Dad said I could ride again while you two are gone."

Trace had been furious when he discovered the pranks Becky had done. He'd restricted her from riding and given her extra chores, including doing all Kalli's paperwork. But he had also listened to the lonely little girl and spent extra hours with her all summer, to show his precious daughter that he still loved her, to reassure her that falling in love with Kalli had not diminished his love for Becky, only enlarged their family.

Kalli had been included in many of the activities, and until now she had thought she and Becky were getting along fine.

"That's good, about riding. Was there something else?" It was almost time to start the ceremony. Her heart began beating faster at the thought of joining her life with Trace's. Was Becky having doubts at this late moment? Did she not want the wedding to take place?

"You and Daddy are marrying soon." Becky glanced at the clock, then back at Kalli.

"Yes, my father will be here any minute and then we'll get this show on the road. Is that a problem?"

Becky shook her head quickly. "I just thought, I mean, I wondered if because you're marrying Daddy you'll be like my mom or something."

"Yes. I'll be your stepmother." Kalli watched her closely. Where was this conversation leading?

"Could I call you Mom?" Becky asked softly, her eyes resting pleadingly on Kalli.

"Oh, sweetheart, of course you can. I would love nothing better." Kalli leaned forward and gathered the preteen into her arms, holding her tightly, tears of happiness glimmering on her lashes. "You are the sweet child of my heart. Even if your dad and I have a dozen kids, I'll never love any of them more than I love you."

Just then Trace pushed open the door.

"Trace, You can't come in here!" Kalli exclaimed, horrified.

"Scat, brat." Motioning to his daughter, he jerked his thumb toward the door. Becky grinned and scooted out. "See you out front, Dad. *Mom.*"

"Mom?" he closed the door behind his daughter.

"Yes. What are you doing here? Don't you know it's bad luck?"

"The only bad luck I've had is that I've had to wait so long to see you again. To kiss you." He crossed the room in three strides, gently gathering her up in his arms, bridal dress, veil and all. "God, sweetheart, you're beautiful." Then his mouth descended and Kalli forgot all about bad luck, the waiting guests and her new daughter. She was consumed by Trace. Her world narrowed until it was only the two of them. Endless delight spiraled through her at his touch. She could float forever in his arms.

He tasted the honey sweetness of her mouth, plunging again and again into her moist warmth. He would never get enough of this woman if they both lived to be a hundred.

He lifted his head and glanced toward her bed.

"Don't even think it," she warned, snuggling closer without a single care about wrinkling her gown.

"These last two months have been murder," he said brushing his lips against hers as if he couldn't bear to be separated.

"It wasn't as if we've been practicing abstinence," she remarked, framing his face and smiling warmly up into his hot eyes.

"Well, I haven't woken up every morning with you in my bed where you belong, either!"

"Starting tomorrow you will," she promised. "Why are you here?"

"To get a couple of good kisses in before the ceremonial peck at the altar. It'll be hours before I can get you alone again. I couldn't wait."

Kalli thrilled once again to his touch, as she always did, and probably always would. She knew she'd have to face the wedding party with her lips swollen and rosy from his embrace, but she wouldn't trade a single second of being in his arms for anything.

Finally he broke the kiss and stepped back, fingering the veil with his roughen fingers. "That will have to hold me, I guess. I'll see you out front?"

"You can count on it, cowboy."

Yeah, I remember, you're in it for the long haul."

She nodded, her eyes shining with happiness and love.

* * * * *

COMING NEXT MONTH

#979 MEGAN'S MARRIAGE—Annette Broadrick
Daughters of Texas
February's *Man of the Month* and Aqua Verde County's most eligible bachelor, Travis Hanes, wanted Megan O'Brien as his bride. And now that she needed his help, could Travis finally talk stubborn Megan into being the wife he wanted?

#980 ASSIGNMENT: MARRIAGE—Jackie Merritt
Tuck Hannigan had to pose as pretty Nicole Currie's husband if he was going to protect her. Could this phony marriage get the confirmed bachelor thinking about a honeymoon for real?

#981 REESE: THE UNTAMED—Susan Connell
Sons and Lovers
Notorious playboy Reese Marchand knew mysteriously sexy Beth Langdon was trouble. But he couldn't stay away from the long-legged beauty—even if it meant revealing his long-kept secret.

#982 THIS IS MY CHILD—Lucy Gordon
Single dad Giles Haverill was the only man who could help Melanie Haynes find the baby she'd been forced to give up years ago. Unfortunately, he was also the one man she could never love....

#983 DADDY'S CHOICE—Doreen Owens Malek
Taylor Kirkland's goal in life was to regain custody of his daughter. But then he met Carol Lansing—an irresistible woman whose love could cost him that dream....

#984 HUSBAND MATERIAL—Rita Rainville
Matthew Flint never thought he would make a good husband—until he lost the only woman he ever loved. Now he would do anything to convince Libby Cassidy he really was husband material.

Take 4 bestselling love stories FREE

Plus get a FREE surprise gift!

Special Limited-time Offer

Mail to Silhouette Reader Service™

> **P.O. Box 609**
> **Fort Erie, Ontario**
> **L2A 5X3**

YES! Please send me 4 free Silhouette Desire® novels and my free surprise gift. Then send me 6 brand-new novels every month, which I will receive months before they appear in bookstores. Bill me at the low price of $2.74 each plus 25¢ delivery and GST*. That's the complete price and a savings of over 10% off the cover prices—quite a bargain! I understand that accepting the books and gift places me under no obligation ever to buy any books. I can always return a shipment and cancel at any time. Even if I never buy another book from Silhouette, the 4 free books and the surprise gift are mine to keep forever.

326 BPA AQS5

Name	(PLEASE PRINT)	
Address	Apt. No.	
City	Province	Postal Code

This offer is limited to one order per household and not valid to present Silhouette Desire® subscribers. *Terms and prices are subject to change without notice. Canadian residents will be charged applicable provincial taxes and GST.

CDES-295   ©1990 Harlequin Enterprises Limited

Bestselling author

Rachel Lee

takes her Conard County series to new heights with

This March, Rachel Lee brings readers a brand-new, longer-length, out-of-series title featuring the characters from her successful Conard County miniseries.

Janet Tate and Abel Pierce have both been betrayed and carry deep, bitter memories. Brought together by great passion, they must learn to trust again.

"Conard County is a wonderful place to visit! Rachel Lee has crafted warm, enchanting stories. These are wonderful books to curl up with and read. I highly recommend them."
— *New York Times* bestselling author
Heather Graham Pozzessere

Available in March, wherever Silhouette books are sold.

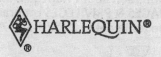

You're About to Become a  *Privileged Woman*

Reap the rewards of fabulous free gifts and benefits with proofs-of-purchase from Silhouette and Harlequin books

Pages & Privileges™

It's our way of thanking you for buying our books at your favorite retail stores.

**Harlequin and Silhouette—
the most privileged readers in the world!**

For more information about Harlequin and Silhouette's PAGES & PRIVILEGES program call the Pages & Privileges Benefits Desk: **1-503-794-2499**

 *Silhouette*®

TM

SD-PP91